THE FIGHT IN US

THE FOUR - BOOK 4

BECCA STEELE

the fight in us

USA TODAY & WALL STREET JOURNAL BESTSELLING AUTHOR

BECCA STEELE

AUTHOR'S NOTE

The author is British, and British English spellings and phrases are used throughout.

For Claudia (again)

Anything worth having is worth fighting for.

— *SUSAN ELIZABETH PHILLIPS*

1

lena

AGE EIGHT

He was here again. The boy with the dark hair and the bright smile.

Weston Cavendish.

I sat back against the wall of the playroom, hugging my knees, the unfinished LEGO next to me forgotten. My older brother, Cassius, and Weston's brother, Caiden, slumped down on the beanbags in front of the TV, ready to play a racing game.

Weston's gaze travelled around the room and landed on me, and that smile appeared on his face. It gave me a funny fluttery feeling in my tummy, and I had to look away from him.

"What ya making?" He came to a stop in front of me, crouching down and staring at my unfinished piece with his head cocked.

"A-a house." My voice came out all scratchy, and my cheeks felt hot as he turned from the LEGO to look at me with his colour-changing eyes. They were like magic. Kind of a deep blue, but with greys and greens swirled in. Like the sea that I saw from the windows of my house every single day.

"Cool. Can I play?" Not waiting for a reply, he took a spare board from the open box next to me and started laying out pieces. We built in silence for a while, just us two in our corner of the room, our brothers occupied by their game.

"What do you wanna be when you grow up?"

His voice made me jump, and the piece of LEGO I'd been holding fell from my hand. "What do *you* wanna be?" I asked him, while I tried to think of an answer that would impress him.

"I want to be like Tony Stark."

I bit my lip. "Who's that?"

He rolled his eyes and huffed. "Iron Man. He has all this cool computer stuff, and he invents robots and things like that. And he defeats villains like Galactus."

My cheeks were getting redder as I looked at him, unsure. "Y-you want to be a superhero?"

"Kind of, yeah." He puffed out his chest, grinning. "A computer superhero."

"Me too." The words slipped out before I could think about them.

His eyes widened. "*You* want to be a computer superhero?"

"Yep." I nodded, trying to sound confident even though I felt sick with nerves. I didn't even have a computer of my own. "I love computers."

His whole face lit up, like I'd never seen before, and my breath caught in my throat as his eyes focused on mine.

"Me too." He repeated the words I'd just said, smiling shyly at me from under his lashes.

That was the moment I knew I'd do whatever it took to keep that boy smiling at me, the way he was right then.

That was the moment I knew I loved Weston Cavendish.

2

weston

e hadn't even been at the party long, and I was already bored out of my mind. My dad, Arlo Cavendish, and stepmother, Christine Clifford, had forced us all to attend. The primary objective was to keep up the charade that we were a happy family, now that my stepsister, Winter Huntington, had moved to the area and was attending Alstone College with us.

My brother, Caiden, and I barely got along with our dad, and with Christine on the scene, being around them was almost intolerable. There was no love lost between Winter and her mother, either. They'd been estranged until recently. Winter had grown up with her dad, John Huntington, who had passed away almost a year ago. Now, she was living here in Alstone.

So here we were—me, Caiden, and Winter, all of us uncomfortable and wishing we could be anywhere else but here in my dad's mansion, surrounded by members of the

Alstone elite and whoever else was currently trying to suck up to my dad and stepmother.

"Hello, beautiful."

Turning from the bar, I watched James Granville, a guy that none of us particularly liked given that he was related to our business rivals (a rivalry that dated back years), greet Winter. She returned his greeting with genuine happiness, throwing her arms around him. Caiden's eyes darkened, and his mouth set in a hard line. As one, we moved to stand on either side of Winter, reminding James of his place.

Although, I was certain that Caiden's hostility towards James had little to do with our family rivalry, and everything to do with our new stepsister. I could pretty much guarantee how this would go down. Cade would get jealous, probably do something like flirt with, or worse, fuck Portia or Jessa or another one of the vapid girls who hung around us at these events, in an attempt to make himself forget, and then get wasted and hate himself.

Yeah, my brother was all kinds of fucked up right now.

"Granville," Caiden growled, and James replied in the same tone, stepping forwards. Internally rolling my eyes, I ignored their dick-measuring contest, my gaze drifting to the girl he'd arrived with.

Lena Drummond. My best friend Cassius' younger sister. All dressed in black, as usual, her long blonde hair loose and poker straight. Something flashed in her blue eyes as they met mine, but it was gone before I could read it, and her face defaulted to its usual unsmiling expression.

Wait. She'd turned up with James Granville. A weird sensation twisted my stomach, something I didn't quite understand. The words came out before I had a chance to think about them. "Lena? What're you doing with Granville?" She held my gaze for a moment, and it looked like she was trying to read something on my face. What, I had no fucking clue. When I remained standing there, waiting for her to explain, she breathed out heavily and rolled her eyes.

"He gave me a lift. Get over it. I'm here—that has to count for something." Before I could say anything in reply, she turned on her heel and disappeared into the crowds.

"Who was that?" Winter asked me curiously.

"Lena Drummond. Cassius' sister. She's seventeen and…mad at the world? Or something? I don't know. She's moody."

"Right." She sighed. "Thanks for your insightful comments, West."

I grinned at her, grabbing my drink from the bar and lifting it to my lips. "Pleasure."

Downing my pint, I tuned out James and Caiden as I scanned the crowd. I caught a flash of blonde hair out of the corner of my eye, and my heart sped up.

What the fuck?

I was interrupted from my thoughts by Winter threading her arm through mine. She smiled up at me. "Shall we go and mingle?"

Yes. I stared in the direction of the blonde head, all the way over the other side of the room, but gave a groan. Couldn't seem too eager. "We'd better. Come on."

By the time we'd made it to the far side of the room, Lena had disappeared.

Hours later, the party was still going strong, but I'd escaped to the relative peace of the study with Cassius and our housemate, Zayde Lowry, who was also my brother's best mate. Cass had dragged a girl in with him, and while I'd normally do the same, I wasn't feeling it tonight for some reason.

"Wanna play?" I suggested to Zayde, already heading over to the dartboard and pulling down a handful of darts.

"Only if we make it interesting."

"Play for money?"

Zayde nodded, and I stepped back from the board. "You go first."

We'd been playing for a while, and it was a fucking miracle, but Zayde was off his game. I was in the lead. This shit needed to be documented, because I doubted it would happen again.

Just when I'd taken my phone out to take a photo of the scoreboard, there was a series of knocks on the door.

"Who's that?"

"How the fuck would I know?" my brother muttered in reply to my pointless question, all sighing and sulky, stomping over to the door to open it. He seriously needed to get laid or something. His brooding anger was on a hair trigger, even more so since Winter had shown up in our lives.

Lena appeared in the room, and I forgot all about the game as I took her in. Dropping her phone to the sofa next to Cassius, she glanced around the room. "Can someone take me home?"

Cassius said something that I didn't hear as I stood rooted to the spot, staring at her, trying to work out what the fuck I was feeling when I looked at this girl. I needed another drink. Lucky for my dart game, but unlucky for me, I'd only had one beer back at the beginning of the night.

"—He can't take me home since he's had a drink. Mum and Dad left ages ago, and I just tried to get an Uber, but they can't come for another forty-five minutes," Lena was saying when my brain finally decided to tune back into the conversation.

I was already moving towards her. "I'll take you."

"No, I'll take her." Zayde appeared next to me, his tone threaded with ice.

I gritted my teeth. "I already offered."

He turned the full force of his icy gaze on me. "I'm taking her."

I glared right back at him, refusing to be the one to break our stand-off.

The stand-off ended with Lena's words. "Sorry, West, but Z has a bike." She stared at me with an unreadable expression on her face, before she twisted the knife by adding, "And I need to feel the power between my legs, if you know what I'm saying."

Then they were gone. Unreasonable jealousy and anger raged inside of me, and I didn't even know why.

"What was all that about, West?" My brother gave me a curious look.

"Nothing." Stalking back over to the dartboard, I grabbed a handful of darts, launching them at the board.

I couldn't shake the haze of anger. "I'm out of here." I threw the final dart, uncaring, and it clattered to the floor.

I needed a drink. Now.

3

lena

I glanced up at my brother, Cassius, as we headed into the bowling alley with our friends Winter and Caiden. "Where's West?" My voice was casual. "I thought he was coming bowling."

"He is." Cassius scanned the large open space. Colourful lights played over the lanes, and music pumped from the speakers, accompanied by the sounds of falling pins. "There."

I followed his line of sight to see Weston propped up against the bar, openly flirting with a gorgeous girl with short, jet-black hair who was waiting to be served. She laughed at something he said, placing her hand on his arm, and I pushed down the unwanted spike of jealousy at her actions.

Weston wasn't mine.

And I had to remember that.

I'd perfected the art of pretending over the years. Pretending I only saw Weston as a friend. Pretending that

11

he didn't affect me. Pretending it didn't cut me up inside every time another new conquest ended up in his bed. Pretending I hadn't been in love with him ever since I was eight years old. Pretending that he'd ever look at me as anything more than his best friend's sister.

Always pretending.

I'd pretended for so long that the pretence had become real.

Almost.

With an effort I turned my back on the bar and faced the bowling lanes. "Ready to be beaten?"

Cassius laughed next to me, then reached over and ruffled my hair. "You wish. I'm unbeatable."

I threw him a warning look, smoothing my hair back down. "We'll see about that."

An hour later, we were about to start a new game, and Cassius and Zayde were tied for first place. Even though Zayde had arrived late, he'd somehow managed to catch up and move into the lead.

Everyone was in a great mood, happy to just be having fun without anything hanging over their heads. Winter and Caiden, especially. Winter had spent months investigating her dad's sudden, suspicious death, and it had led her to Alstone, where it had turned out that her own mother was the one behind it. Add in betrayal from Allan, a guy that had been really close to the entire Cavendish family, and involvement with a Belarusian gang...let's just say, we could all breathe more easily these days now that it was all behind us.

And another bonus? I had a new friend, Winter, and

Caiden had finally stopped acting like an angry, moody bastard now that he was all loved-up with her.

"I'll be back." I waved my hand in the direction of the toilets. "Anyone want more drinks while I'm up?"

"I'll get them." Winter smiled at me. "Meet you at the bar in a few."

Exiting the loos, I headed back down the corridor, taking the chance to check my phone in case there was anything that needed my attention. Clearly, I wasn't paying attention, because I ran straight into someone, my phone falling from my grip and clattering to the floor.

Not *someone*.

Weston.

His arm shot out, his hand gripping my elbow to steady me. "Fuck, sorry. I wasn't looking where I was going." Dipping down, he swiped my phone from the floor before straightening up.

"Doesn't look broken." He turned it over in his grip, smoothing his thumb over the screen, then handed it back to me.

His sudden presence had flustered me, and I stood there mutely like an idiot, just staring at him. As the silence stretched, his lips curved upwards in amusement. "Everything okay?"

"Um." I licked my lips, and his eyes darted down, following my movements. "Yeah. I'm fine," I managed to say, my voice coming out all hoarse for some stupid reason.

Now it was his turn for silence. He continued to stare at my mouth through lowered lashes, and my skin grew hot as I realised that he was still holding on to my arm.

The sound of footsteps coming down the corridor broke the spell, and he blinked, dropping his grip on me. He turned away without another word, leaving me staring after him.

What was that?

Back in the bowling alley, I joined Winter at the bar, where she was ordering large jugs of beer to share, plus Coke for the drivers. "Should we get snacks?" she mused as I came to stand next to her.

I shook off the weird moment I'd just had with West and attempted to act normal. "Yeah. Everyone always wants snacks."

"True." With a laugh, she glanced over at me, then frowned. "Are you okay?"

"Why wouldn't I be?" My voice came out more defensive than I'd planned, and she raised a brow.

"Just asking. You look a bit...flushed. Are you feeling okay?"

I forced a laugh and repeated the words I'd just spoken to Weston, not meaning them this time, either. "Yeah, I'm fine." As Winter eyed me, unconvinced, I added, "Just a bit hot. I could do with a cold drink."

She seemed to accept that as an explanation, indicating her head towards the beer that the bartender had just placed in front of us. "I've got you covered there. I'll just order some snacks, then you can help me carry the drinks back over."

"Curly fries. And Cajun wedges?"

"Yep." She nodded, then placed the additional order. "Come on. Let's try and beat the boys. I'm pretty sure we can throw them off their game."

"How?" I stared at her, intrigued.

"Distract them?"

"How?" I repeated.

"I'm sure we'll think of something."

We didn't manage to throw them off their game. Winter's "distraction" techniques, which involved getting Cassius to tell jokes and flirting like mad with Cade, were an epic fail. After three games, Caiden ended up as the overall winner, and Cassius had moved into second place, with Zayde in third.

I was normally fairly good at bowling, as was Weston, but there seemed to be a bit of awkwardness in both of us after our moment in the corridor. I could've been projecting, in fact, I was 90 percent sure I was, but we were both distracted and playing badly.

The tiniest spark of hope sprang to life inside me.

It remained until we were leaving the bowling alley. The girl who West had been flirting with earlier was standing close to the exit, and as we made our way outside, she curled her finger at him with a sultry smile on her face.

When he broke away from our group, heading in her direction, I didn't wait to see anything else. I rushed outside as quickly as I could, swallowing the feelings that I knew I couldn't afford to have for him.

Weston Cavendish would never be mine.

4

weston

My computer pinged with a message alert, then another. Mercury and Xenon.

Navigating to Xenon's first, I rubbed my brow. Bloody headache.

Xenon: Yes I'm a genius. All done

Yes. The job had been a tricky one, but between me and Xenon, we'd done it. The assignment had come from Xenon's boss, and the weird thing was, the client was none other than my dad, Arlo. Did he know I was the one dealing with it? I wasn't sure, but I knew not to underestimate him. Whether my dad knew it was me or not, fuck it. I'd do what I needed to do. In this instance, the assignment involved looking into the background of the head finance guy at Alstone Holdings, Mr. Martin Smith.

Alstone Holdings was the company that was founded by three families—mine, the Drummond family, and the Lowry family. Primarily in construction and land acquisition, they owned most of the land and property in Alstone and the surrounding area and had far-reaching business connections that stretched across the country and even internationally.

Something about this particular employee had thrown up red flags—my dad had suspicions around discrepancies in the accounts, numbers that hadn't been adding up—and although this guy had an explanation for everything, my dad wasn't convinced. He wanted to pin something on him legally but wasn't above illegal methods to do so, which was where I came in. I was supposed to be looking out for anything that would stand out as suspicious. That didn't give me much to go on, but I wasn't going to let that stop me.

How did I get involved in all this shit to begin with? It had happened when I was playing with my newfound set of skills and had managed to break into Kryptos, a legendary hidden system deep within the dark web. About half a second after I'd been greeted with a flashing *K* symbol, my entire network had been taken over by an unknown controller. Nothing worked, and I'd fucking panicked, watching helplessly as my system destroyed itself before my eyes. Me, a cocky sixteen-year-old, thinking I was this invincible genius hacker, until I wasn't.

Half an hour after it had happened, my system was back online as if nothing had happened, complete with a message on my screen and a link to a hidden portal on the dark web. Within the portal, I'd been given various tests, and afterwards, my formal offer of employment. Hacking into Kryptos had been a test of skills, and apparently, I'd passed.

All of us were anonymous, assigned code names when we began working for Promethium. Hence my nickname, Nitro. Over the years I'd been doing it, I'd come to know my colleague-slash-fellow hacker Mercury...not *know*, exactly, but we'd built a kind of online friendship, and we trusted one another and helped each other out. Then there was Xenon, higher in ranking than us, and above him was Promethium. There was a huge network of us out there, all working for Promethium and collectively known as Kryptos, but I only really interacted with Mercury and Xenon.

Back to my current task. My dad had asked us to look into this guy's background and go through his correspondence to see if there was anything that would connect him to the discrepancies in the company finances. Problem was, the fucker had a level of encryption on his phone that I couldn't manage to get through, so I'd asked Xenon to help. Not that he'd do anything for free—no, he wanted an undisclosed future favour in return. Something I'd probably end up regretting, knowing him.

Leaving my computer to filter through the data from the guy's phone, I headed for the kitchen to grab a drink. My housemate and best friend, Cassius, was already there, thumbing through his phone, and he looked up with a grin as I entered.

"Alright, mate? You done with your computer shit already?"

"Nope." Swiping a bottle of water from the fridge, I thought about it for a minute. Fuck it. It could take hours for the software to analyse all the data on the phone, depending on how many emails and messages he had. And my headache was getting worse. "Actually, yeah, I am. You wanna head out?"

"Always ready." He bounded up from his stool, grabbing his keys from the island, and headed around to meet me.

"Where's everyone else?" The house seemed quieter than usual.

"Cade and Z are working out in the basement. Winter's at uni, said she'd meet us when we were ready."

"Okay. Just gonna check a message from Mercury before we go." I stopped in front of the door to the computer room, but Cass grabbed my arm to pull me away.

"Leave it. It'll still be there when we get back."

True. He hadn't sent me an alert, which would've indicated it was urgent. Whatever it was could wait.

"You're right."

"Always am."

Rolling my eyes at his words, I followed him out of the door.

"Best of three?" Cassius didn't even wait for my reply before racking up the pool balls again.

Placing my beer down on the high table next to me, I wiped my mouth with the back of my hand before replying. "Yeah." We were in the Student Union bar, after the world's quickest trip to the campus library to pick up some books. My workload was heavier this semester, and I was juggling it with my part-time job doing IT support right here at Alstone College. The job was easy, and it was additional experience for the future. But it was an added time suck, especially now I had this additional assignment for Kryptos.

Still, there wasn't really any need to worry. My classes were easy...all other than economics, but I had Winter to help me. Now she was living with us, we'd fallen into the habit of going through my economics coursework in the evenings in front of the TV.

Speaking of Winter...

"Doubles?"

I looked up from my pool cue to see her grinning at me. I returned her smile as she swung her bag from her shoulder, dropping it to the floor.

My smile dropped as I saw Winter's friend Kinslee next to her, shuffling her feet. Fuck. Things had become a bit strained between the two of us, and I knew it was my fault. We'd slept together once when we were both drunk, and I knew she wanted a repeat. The problem was my dick wasn't interested. My gaze swept over her, taking in her tumbling curls, curvy body, and huge eyes. Nope. Not even a flicker of interest.

"My two favourite girls." Cassius came around the table, pulling them both into a hug, and just like that, the tension was broken. Maybe it was all in my head. It had been months since everything had gone down between us, anyway.

As Cassius finally released her, her eyes met mine, and now I could clearly see there was only friendliness in her warm gaze.

Fuck. I didn't understand women. Despite the fact that I had my fair share of female interest, it seemed like I was still no better at reading the signs. Not to sound arrogant, but I'd never really had to. Women came to me—one of the perks of being one of the Four. The Four being me, Caiden, Cassius, and Zayde. Fuck knows who had even started calling us that, but it had stuck, and that was what we were collectively known as. We even had tattoos of the number 4 in Roman numerals. Winter did too, now that she was officially one of us.

Whatever the reason was, I hadn't had to work for female attention.

I smirked to myself, which Winter caught. "Something

funny?" She studied me as she chalked her pool cue, then blew on it.

"Not really. Just thinking that I'll never understand women."

Cassius slung his arm over my shoulder. "Mate, don't even try." With that sage advice, he removed his arm, leaning over the table and angling his pool cue. "Boys versus girls. Loser makes dinner."

"Why is it always about food with you?" Winter took her turn at the table, sending a striped ball flying into the corner pocket.

"I'm a growing boy."

My phone buzzed with a message alert, and I took it out while I waited for my turn at the table.

"Yes!"

Everyone turned to me at my shout.

"Didn't mean to shout. My car's ready. I can pick it up tomorrow morning."

"Want me to drop you at the garage? I can miss my Economics class." Cass had a huge grin on his face. He knew, better than anyone, just how much I'd been looking forward to this day. My own car at last. Not just any car, either. An Aston Martin DBS Superleggera, thanks to my dad's newfound friendship with his new business associate, Lars De Witt. I'd been on the ridiculously long waiting list for another Aston Martin model, but when my dad offered me this car via Lars, there was no way I was going to turn it down. It was a year old, but it had spent most of its life so far sitting in a garage, and that was a crime I couldn't ignore. I'd just been waiting on the custom matte-black paint job, and now, it was finally ready.

"Nah, I'll get an Uber. Thanks, though."

"You know what this means. We need to celebrate your

new wheels. Friday night." My best mate was already tapping on his phone. "I heard that whatshername's single now. Laura? I think?"

I thought about it for a minute. "Yeah, invite her, and her friend. The one with the dark hair."

"Would you say you prefer girls with dark hair?" Winter was suddenly in my face, studying me intently.

"What? Why?" I raised a brow. "I don't have a type."

She nodded, then abruptly turned away, dismissing me. Shaking my head, I lined my cue up, ready to sink the ball into the middle pocket before tapping the white ball lightly. Perfect shot.

"Hey, Cass? You're inviting Lena," I heard Winter say, as I sank another ball. He said something in reply that was too low for me to hear over the noise of the bar.

Lena Drummond.

The girl I never allowed myself to think about.

The one single girl who was completely off limits.

My best friend's sister.

5

weston

E arly the following morning, before anyone else was up, I unlocked the door to the computer room and headed over to my desk. A bank of monitors faced me, most of them dark, but one was lit up and scrolling through our various security feeds. The other was flashing a message at me.

Analysis Complete

Thank fuck for Xenon. The program he'd written and sent to me was insane. It scanned all the hacked data, using various algorithms to flag up anything that could be classed as suspicious. While I could've gone through it all manually, the guy had thousands of emails and messages on his phone, and it would've taken me forever.

My headache returned as I started manually sifting through the flagged items. A blinking dot at the corner of the screen reminded me that I had an unread message from Mercury, and I logged in to our encrypted chat.

Mercury: WYR have a frog's legs or a fly's head?

A grin stretched over my face. I couldn't remember who started it first, but in between all the tech shit we talked about, we'd somehow fallen into a habit of throwing these weird as fuck "would you rather" questions at each other at random times.

Me: WTF. How can I answer that?

Even though it was early, not even 6:00 a.m., he was online and replied straight away.

Mercury: Pick one
Me: You're a sadist. OK frog legs I guess. I could hide them under clothes. You?
Mercury: Same. Could be useful
Me: Did Xenon send you the beta program?
Mercury: No. Dickhead wouldn't give it up without a favour
Me: It's good. Saving me fuckloads of time
Mercury: Is fuckloads a word?
Me: Are you the grammar police, hacker boy?
Mercury: Fuck off
Me: OK I've got one. WYR give up your phone or your computer?
Mercury: Damn. I'll get back to you

I signed off, satisfied that I'd managed to stump him temporarily, and returned to sifting through the flagged data from Xenon's program.

"Morning." I was interrupted a while later by the door swinging open. Caiden stepped into the room, balancing a plate in one hand and a mug in the other. "Car day today." He grinned at me, pleased.

"I know. It's taken forever, but I'm glad it worked out. This car's gonna be fucking beautiful."

"But not as good as mine." Smirking, he came to a stop next me and placed the mug and plate on my desk, pushing my keyboard back to make room.

"Mind the keyboard. It's new." I gave him a warning look, making him roll his eyes. "There's no comparison with the cars. Mine's far superior."

"Keep telling yourself that." He pushed the plate towards me. "Breakfast. Eat."

"Thanks." I picked up the bagel, taking a large bite.

"You're welcome. Wanna take our cars for a drive later? Mack's—"

"Fuck, no. I'm not taking my new Aston Martin to that shit excuse for a racetrack. Have you seen the surface? There's more potholes than..." I cast around for a comparison. "Something really potholey."

He raised a brow. "Never took you for a snob."

"I'm not a snob. Just don't want to total my car the first day I get it."

A laugh burst out of him. "Fair enough. Since you won't race, we can agree that I win by default."

"If that's what you want to tell yourself."

After an unsuccessful few hours sifting through Martin Smith's data and finding nothing, not even a hint of anything shady, my mood was low, to say the least. The Uber ride to the garage passed in a blur. The cab driver made small talk, but I couldn't even say what the conversation had been about.

As soon as we pulled up at the garage, I saw the DBS Superleggera in the centre of the forecourt, all matte-black paint and black rims. Finally, my mood improved. Temporarily forgetting my stresses, a huge smile spread across my face as I left the cab and headed straight for my new car, trailing my hand over the smooth metal surface.

Fuck, yeah.

Joe, the forecourt manager, came out to greet me, and I followed him into his office.

"Morning." He took a seat behind his desk, shuffling his paperwork before he slid a slim folder across the surface. "Just these few bits to sign, then she's all yours." Handing me a pen, he sat back while I read through everything.

The paperwork was completed in a few minutes, since we'd done most of it before the respray, and finally, I had the keys in hand, and the Aston Martin was officially all mine.

At last.

"Take good care of her. She's a beauty, mate." Joe patted the top of my car. "Runs like a dream."

"I will."

Leaving the garage forecourt behind me, I grinned at the low rumble of the engine thrumming through my body and the barely harnessed power of the car under my hands. I needed to get this baby out on the open roads so I could see what it was made of. This had been a long time coming.

My phone rang as I was driving back towards Alstone, and Cassius' voice came through the speakers.

"How's the car?"

"Better than yours and Cade's," I told him, just to wind him up.

"Yeah, yeah, whatever you say." I just knew he was

rolling his eyes at me. He cleared his throat. "Can you do me a favour?"

"What is it?" I changed lanes smoothly, noticing the admiring glance of the driver of the car I overtook.

"Can you pick Lena up from school?"

Lena. I'd managed not to think about her, but lately it was growing difficult to ignore her. Now she was friends with Winter, and she'd been involved in the whole business with Winter's mother...she'd been around a lot more often.

Too often.

I wasn't fucking immune. I had eyes and a dick, both of which liked the view.

But I couldn't think of her that way.

Cassius was still speaking. "Her car's in the garage, and I said I'd pick her up, but I've got a meeting with my economics professor that I can't get out of. The fucker just dropped it on me." His displeasure was clear from his tone. "Sorry, mate. I know you just got your new car, but I can't get hold of Winter."

"Yeah, don't worry about it." I stayed casual. I was just doing a favour for my best mate's sister. That was it. "Tell her to meet me out the front." Disconnecting the call, I took the exit to Alstone, heading in the direction of my old school, Alstone High.

6

lena

Waiting on the stone steps outside my school, leaning against one of the stone pillars that flanked the entrance, I scanned the road. All I had was a text from my brother to say he couldn't pick me up, but he'd sorted a lift.

"Are you sure you don't want us to wait with you?" My friend Raine peered up at me from where she was tucked under her boyfriend Carter's arm.

"Do I look like the kind of person that needs someone to wait with me?" I raised a brow. Her reply was lost as the low growl of an engine cut through all the conversations.

"Fuck." There was approval in Carter's voice as we watched a matte-black car pull up, expensive-looking and sexy, if you liked that kind of thing. For me, cars were something to get you from A to B.

Okay, maybe I was a *tiny* bit impressed.

The car was forgotten as the driver pulled to a stop and climbed out, and my mouth went dry. With his attention focused on the crowd of students swarming around him, I let my eyes drink him in from head to toe, despite my brain flashing up warning signs. From his Nikes, up over his faded, ripped jeans, up over his grey T-shirt that clung to his lean, toned torso, up to his angular jaw, past the sunglasses that covered his amazing eyes, and stopping on his dark, almost black hair that was tousled like he'd been running his hand through it.

Wait. Did I just think his eyes were amazing?

I huffed and snapped my gaze away.

"What's Weston Cavendish doing here?" Carter started down the steps, tugging Raine with him, and I had no choice but to follow.

I swallowed hard. "I think...I think he's here for me," I muttered.

"Nice wheels" was the first thing Carter said when we reached Weston. A blinding grin spread across Weston's face, and even though it wasn't directed at me, I shivered.

No.

I'd perfected the art of pretending that Weston didn't affect me over the years, and I wasn't about to break now.

Affixing a bored expression on my face, I turned to Raine as Carter and Weston started talking about torque and engine shit.

"He's even better-looking than I remembered." Raine nudged me with her elbow.

"Is he?"

Maybe my mask was flimsier than I realised, because she wasn't fooled by my false nonchalance. "You know, I remember you hanging out with him a bit last year when he was still at school with us."

"We didn't 'hang out.' Maybe I spoke to him sometimes —he's my brother's best friend, after all. But he was the football team captain, and you know how I feel about the popular crowd."

She arched her brow, clearly unconvinced. "Yet you sit with them every day at lunch."

"Only because your boyfriend is the team captain," I shot back.

"You love them really. Don't even pretend." Glancing over at her boyfriend, she gave him a small, private smile.

I hummed non-committally, because maybe they weren't so bad. Not now I'd got to know them.

My eyes strayed to Weston again, despite myself, and my stomach fluttered.

The conversation stopped.

His gaze swung to mine, and he directed that smile at me.

My defences melted away, as if they'd never existed.

Fuck.

I knew he was going to be my downfall. He was going to ruin me.

I'd managed to avoid the fire for so long, but now?

Now I was craving the burn.

I couldn't give in. Weston was a temptation that I couldn't afford.

"Ready to go?" He twirled his keys around on his finger as he continued to disarm me with his smile.

Deep breath. You don't want him. Nodding, I walked around to the passenger side of the car and opened the door, back to my usual confident self.

"Oh. This is nice." My black-tipped fingernails trailed appreciatively over the buttery soft leather of my seat. Clipping my seat belt into place, I took in the interior, all understated elegance and luxury.

"Yeah." The pride in Weston's voice made me smile. Starting up the engine, he casually rested one hand on the steering wheel and the other on the back of my seat as he reversed. When he removed his hand, his fingers caught in my hair.

"Sorry." His voice was soft. His fingertips slid over the strands that rested against my cheek, sending shivers racing through me. "I like your hair this pink colour," he murmured.

Suddenly, it felt like all the air had been sucked from the car. And now I was fucking *blushing*. What the fuck?

He pulled away his hand so fast that it was practically a blur, gripping the steering wheel tightly. I was sure this car hadn't been this small when I got in. Why was I finding it hard to breathe?

As he drove us in the direction of my house, it became apparent that the stifling atmosphere in the car wasn't only caused by whatever weird moment had happened between us. Glancing over at him, I noticed the tight set of his jaw and tension radiating from his body.

"Are you okay?" I ventured, then immediately clamped my mouth shut, instantly regretting speaking up. Surprisingly, though, he answered me.

"Yeah. I…" There was the world's longest pause before he finally continued. "I'm fine. Just got some shit going on. Picking up this baby—" He patted the steering wheel. "—made me forget for a bit, but now…" His shoulders slumped.

What was I supposed to say to that? "Well, that's cryptic." I licked my dry lips. "Um."

Thankfully, he didn't wait for me to attempt to formulate more of a reply, because he gave a loud sigh and turned to me briefly. "Fuck it. It's not important. Just got a lot on my plate. I'll work it out. Are you in a rush to get home?"

"No…"

His hand smoothed over the steering wheel. "Wanna see what this baby is capable of?"

A grin spread across my face. "Yeah. Although I'm kind of concerned by the way you keep referring to it as your baby."

"It *is* my baby." A smile tugged at the corners of his lips, and the whole atmosphere lightened.

"If you say so."

We hit the open clifftop road, and he let the car fly. Now I got it. I got why Winter was so obsessed with Caiden and his car. Seeing Weston handle this powerful machine with ease, his muscles flexing as his hands curved around the steering wheel...there was something so masculine and sexy about it.

I couldn't afford to think that way. I yanked my head around so fast that I was surprised I hadn't given myself whiplash, fixing my gaze on the sea instead.

He directed me to put some music on, so I hooked my phone up to his car system and hit one of my playlists.

"You're an NF fan, hey?" A grin tugged at his lips.

"What gave it away?"

His grin widened, and my stomach flipped again.

I was *so* fucked.

Although the music was relatively slow and we were in a fast car, it somehow fit perfectly. Closing my eyes, I rested my head against the seat.

"Lena?" Blinking my eyes open, I realised that we'd stopped outside my house. Turning to meet Weston's amused gaze, I opened my mouth.

"I think I fell asleep."

"Yeah. I think you did."

He raised his hand and brushed a strand of hair off the side of my face.

My breath caught in my throat.

Confusion filled his eyes, and he dropped his hand immediately, like he'd touched me unthinkingly and was now second-guessing himself. To save things from becoming even more awkward, I quickly unclipped my seat belt and slid out of the car.

"Bye," I said breathlessly, turning and heading for my front door without a backwards glance.

My cheek still burned where he'd touched me.

7

weston

Friday night was my new-car party.

Who the fuck would decide to throw a party for a new car? Cassius Drummond, that was who.

The music was thumping through the house, and I was in the mood to get wasted and find a hot girl to bury myself inside. I still hadn't made any headway on the Martin Smith issue, I'd had a full-on week of studying, and my part-time job in the Alstone College IT department had just brought added pressure that I didn't need. At least I was only doing four hours a week on that, but it was still four hours that I couldn't really spare at the moment. My headaches had been flaring up too. In short, I wasn't the most fun person to be around at this point in time.

"Mate, you okay?" Cassius studied me with a look of concern as I stood leaning against the kitchen counter. This wasn't good. I wasn't about to bring down the mood of the party.

"I need a drink."

"Beer?"

"Something stronger. Much stronger."

A slow smile spread across his face. "Leave it with me."

"Want to go upstairs?"

I blinked as Cindy? Candy? trailed her lips across my ear, pressing her body into mine suggestively.

"Not now, Cindy," I slurred. What I needed was for the room to stop spinning.

"It's Amy, you wanker." She shoved at my chest, pushing away from me, and I groaned as the room spun again. Placing my hand on the wall for balance, I staggered in the direction of the hallway. No destination in mind, but my body seemed to think it was a good idea. Somehow, I ended up in a corner of the lounge area, which was weirdly quiet. Dimly, I remembered people heading outside since it was a warm evening.

I sank into one of the chairs and rested my heavy head in the palms of my hands, willing my head to stop spinning.

"What's wrong?" The soft voice had me dropping my hands, and my gaze trailed up long legs covered in black thigh-high socks and over a pair of black leather shorts topped with a studded silver belt. I didn't get any further before my hands shot out and gripped the girl around the backs of her thighs, pulling her into my lap. I vaguely registered her surprised squeal as my fingers touched her smooth skin, and then I raised my blurry gaze to meet her face.

Oh. *Fuck.*

I buried my face in her soft pink hair as my arms went around her body, hugging her to me. Maybe if I didn't look at her, I could pretend this wasn't real.

"Your hair smells like candy floss," I mumbled, inhaling deeply.

"What the fuck? Are you sniffing my hair?"

"Are you really here?"

This time a laugh escaped her, and she reached between us to grip my chin, forcibly tugging my head upwards.

I leaned back against the armchair headrest with a sigh and closed my eyes but kept my arms around her. The next moment, I felt a sharp pinch on my arm. "Ow! What was that for?"

"You asked if I was really here."

I opened my eyes and groaned at the amusement in Lena's gaze. Had I ever noticed how blue her eyes were before?

"Why are we sitting like this?" She waved a hand between us.

"You're the one sitting on me."

"Like I had any choice." I didn't see her making any effort to move, though. "Just how much did you drink?"

"Dunno. Ask Cass."

She muttered something about her "irresponsible brother" and something about a shiv, but I was lost, my eyes falling closed again as the room continued to spin.

The next thing I was aware of was someone shaking my shoulder. Opening my eyes again, I saw Lena holding out a large glass with some kind of icy-looking brownish liquid and a straw poking out of the top. "Drink this." She handed the glass to me, and I took a tentative taste.

Iced coffee. Strong. Suddenly, I was really thirsty. "Thanks."

She gave me a brief smile, then disappeared.

The coffee worked its magic. Half an hour later, I was definitely still drunk, but I wasn't seeing double. I guessed

I'd been out of it for longer than I thought, because the house was noticeably emptier than it had been, and the music was playing at a volume that meant I didn't have to shout to be heard. Making my way into the kitchen, I poured myself a pint of water, then knocked it back, noticing Cassius heading towards me, for once without a girl all over him.

"Lost your touch, Cass? Not getting any tonight?"

He raised a brow at me. "I could say the same about you."

I shrugged. "Yeah, well." My voice turned serious without me meaning it to. "I've got a lot on my mind."

He gave me that same look of concern he'd given me at the beginning of the night, so I added, "Fuck it. Let's find... Laura, was it? And her friend?"

"Yeah." A grin spread across his face, and he tapped his bottle against my empty pint glass. "Last I saw, they were outside."

A flash of pink hair appeared in my peripheral vision, and I paused. "You go on out. I just wanna check something."

"Alright." He sauntered out of the sliding doors onto the deck, and I heard his "Hi, ladies" and a high-pitched squeal. I doubted he'd even notice if I was there or not.

Instead of following him out, I trailed behind the girl with the pink hair like the stalker that I was, all the way through the house and out of the front door.

What the fuck I was doing, I didn't know.

Call it temporary insanity. Something was pulling me towards her, and I didn't know why. All I knew was, I needed to be near her.

She paused next to the driver's-side door of her car,

turning around to face me. Her expression was impossible to read. "You can stop following me now."

"Where are you going, Lena?" I came to a stop right in front of her, our bodies almost touching.

"H-home." Her voice came out all breathy.

"Why?" I planted one hand against the door of her car, next to her shoulder, and the other...fuck, I guess I was still drunk because it had a mind of its own, trailing up her arm. "Why?" I asked again, lowering my voice and dipping my head to run my nose down her cheek.

Her breath hitched, and her lips parted. "You're drunk," she managed.

"Not that drunk."

"Drunk enough." With a sudden surge of energy, she straightened up, giving me a shove backwards. I stumbled on the gravel, caught off guard. Before I could recover, she slipped inside her car, locking the doors.

She sped away without a backwards look, and I went back inside, suddenly feeling way too sober and no longer in the mood to party.

Instead, I went to bed. Alone.

8

mercury

My fingers moved swiftly across the keys, navigating to the dark web chat room. After traversing the outer levels of security, I input the final password, and I was in.

I bypassed Xenon's blinking message alert; he could wait. Instead, I clicked on Nitro's name to open a new chat. I hesitated for a moment. Was I doing the right thing?

No. He had the right to know. As soon as I'd hacked into the footage from Alstone Docks and processed the video until the audio was clear, I knew I couldn't sit on this.

There was the small chance that he might work out who I was, but I'd been careful to cover my tracks. Here in the hidden depths of the dark web, we remained completely anonymous, communicating on a regular basis but never revealing anything that could identify us in the outside world.

Not that Weston Cavendish would suspect who I was. No one would.

I typed out a message, short and to the point.

Mercury: Thought you deserved to see this.

I attached the file, then hit Send and sat back. Waiting for the fallout.

9

weston

After a night of very little sleep, I stumbled downstairs, my eyes gritty and my stomach churning. After making a coffee, I made my way to the computer room to see if Xenon's program had come up with anything useful. Nothing new, but there was a message waiting for me.

Mercury: Thought you deserved to see this.

There was a video file attached, and I clicked to open it. And my whole world came crashing down.

I replayed the video, over and over again, attempting to make sense of it all. Footage from the docks where my brother had been shot by our crazy as fuck stepmother, Christine, earlier in the year. He'd survived, but she hadn't, and that was the only good thing to come out of that fucking nightmare.

Despite the image being grainy and fuzzy, thanks to the darkness and the stormy conditions, the audio was clear. Christine's voice played on repeat in my head, over and over again.

"One Cavendish down, three to go. I was originally going to let the boys live, but after tonight...no. I'm afraid I can't risk keeping them alive."

"One Cavendish down?" Winter had replied, her voice full of horror.

"Arlo's wife was easy. The right words whispered in her ear, the open bottle of pills...I barely had to do anything."

I'd always been told that my mum had died from a brain haemorrhage, but Christine's words seemed to imply that something else had happened. Why hadn't Winter or Caiden mentioned this to me? Both of them had clearly heard. It wasn't like they hadn't had time to bring it up, either. Months had passed since that whole thing went down.

I made another coffee on autopilot, glad that no one else was around yet. What was I supposed to say? Just come out and ask my brother if he'd been lying to me all this time? Or was it Christine's sick way of trying to cause yet more rifts between us?

First up, I needed to do some digging. Get into the death records and find out just what the fuck was going on. The other thought running through my mind was the mystery of Mercury's identity. He'd never given any indication that he knew me, but his actions were completely out of character. For him to send me that particular bit of footage had to mean that he knew me personally.

That meant he had an advantage over me. And until I found out who he was, I couldn't trust him.

I sent him a message, which I doubted he'd reply to, but I had to try.

Me: Who are you?

Surprisingly, he actually responded. To say I was shocked was a fucking understatement. Until I read his reply, which told me nothing.

Mercury: Someone who thinks you deserve the truth
Me: Do I know you?

He went offline then and didn't reappear again.

Leaving Mercury to one side, because I had enough shit to deal with as it was, I turned my attention to the more important issue of hacking into the records. Two hours later, and I had my answer. The coroner's report had been sealed, and my mum's official death record simply stated the cause of death as a brain haemorrhage caused by an accidental overdose.

Three words flashed up from the coroner's report, burning into my brain. Breathing deeply through the nausea until I was more or less sure I wasn't about to lose the contents of my stomach, I stared at the screen, willing it to change.

Suicide. Opiate overdose.

Had my dad known? He must have. I needed to speak to him, the sooner the better.

The day I'd found out about my mum rose in my mind, and I leaned back in my chair, lost in the memory.

"Weston?" My dad's terse voice sounded through my phone. "Be ready to leave in five minutes. I'm on my way."

The call abruptly cut off, and I stared down at my now-blank screen. "Sorry, mate." I turned to my friend Rumi. "My dad's coming to pick me up."

"What? We haven't even played my new computer game yet."

"I know. Sorry." I shrugged, annoyance filling me. "I don't know why, but you know what my dad's like. No point arguing with him."

Rumi's mouth twisted. "Yeah. See you at school on Monday, I guess." He kicked at the grass dejectedly for a minute before his face brightened. "Quick one-on-one while we're waiting for your dad?"

I hopped off the wall I'd been sitting on and ran to the football lying on the grass before Rumi could get to it. He laughed, racing after me, and I lost myself in our competitive game.

For four minutes, everything was fine. Normal.

Then my dad showed up, and everything changed.

I buried my head in my hands, trying to think about anything except that day.

I couldn't stop the memories from assaulting me.

. . .

The gates to our house were wide open, flashing lights from police cars and an ambulance lighting up the growing darkness, illuminating the stone walls of the house and turning them blue.

"D-dad? What's going on?" My voice shook. He didn't answer me, instead climbing out of the car and heading towards one of the police officers standing outside.

My eyes darted to the open front door of the house, and I noticed a figure on the steps.

My brother, Caiden.

Sitting with his knees pulled up, his head was buried in his arms. A blanket had been draped over his shoulders, but I could see that he was shivering as I neared him.

"Cade?"

He raised his head, and I sucked in a breath. His face was drained of colour, his eyes red-rimmed and devastated. "M-mum's..." was all he managed to scrape out, before his eyes filled with tears and he dropped his head in his arms again, his shoulders shaking.

I sank down onto the steps next to him and slipped my arm around his shoulder, trying to comfort my big brother as he fell apart.

The next week passed in a blur. My dad's words kept echoing over and over in my head. "Your mother has passed away." He was withdrawn, blank, shutting himself in his office for hours. Caiden was the same, hiding away in his room. I wandered the silent house, hurting and alone, constantly replaying the last time I'd seen my mum on the morning of her death. She'd been withdrawn, sad, for a long time now, but that morning, she seemed lighter than she'd been in so long. She'd made me toast, singing along with the radio and chatting to me about my schoolwork. When I left for school, she'd wrapped me in her arms and kissed my cheek. "I love you, Weston. Never forget that."

That was the last time I saw her alive.

I'd give anything for just one more moment with her.

When the post-mortem results came, my dad sat me down, exchanging a long, loaded look with my brother.

"Your mother's death was an accident. A brain haemor-rhage. Could have happened to anyone, at any time. There was nothing any of us could have done."

Our family was fractured beyond repair. And when my dad moved Christine Clifford into our home, the cracks became a chasm too wide to bridge.

Fuck. I took a deep breath. Losing my mum had been the worst experience of my life, but to now find out that her death hadn't been an accident? That she'd been driven to suicide? And my dad's deceased ex-wife, Christine, had played a part in it?

Why had they lied to me?

The day dragged on while I waited for everyone to return home. Caiden had taken Winter out for the day, Cassius had gone out early to pick up Lena for some family thing, and fuck knew where Zayde was.

The need to confront my brother was so strong, yet I tamped it down. I could understand him wanting to put the whole situation behind him, since he was shot and all that shit, but there was no reason why he should have kept Christine's revelation from me. I knew I needed to give him a chance to explain, though, so I had to be patient. Until then...

I poured myself a drink.

And another.

And another.

Until the memories were softened and blurred, dulled by the alcohol.

In the kitchen, I'd just finished up my fifth—or was it sixth?—drink, when I heard the sound of voices. Cassius appeared in the doorway and took one look at me, then came racing over. "What's wrong? Anything I can do? Want me to beat the shit out of someone? Or set Z on them?"

Despite myself, I laughed. "Nah, but thanks for the offer. I need...I need to speak to Cade and Winter." My eyes fell closed as I leaned against the kitchen island, folding my arms across the cool surface and burying my head in my hands.

The sound of footsteps grew more distant, then closer again. There was a low murmur of voices.

"West?" A hand gently rested on my back, and I raised myself, turning to face Winter as she studied me, worry written all over her face. Caiden came up to stand next to her, slipping his hand around her waist, and she leaned into him.

"Why didn't either of you tell me that Christine had driven my mum to suicide?" The words were out before I could even think about them.

Caiden blanched, jumping back as if he'd been electrocuted. I would've almost found it funny, if I hadn't been watching the sheer panic appear in his eyes. My confident older brother was suddenly lost for words.

"Can you explain what you mean by that?" Winter spoke carefully, and I nodded, trying to push away the hurt for a minute so I could concentrate on what I was saying.

"I've seen footage from the docks. I heard Christine say to you both that—that." My voice cracked, and I took a deep breath. *Fuck.* I couldn't lose it now. "I heard her say that she encouraged Mum to commit suicide."

My brother's wide, panicked gaze swung to Winter's, and a dawning realisation gripped me. His usual mask was gone, and I could read him perfectly.

"You knew already, didn't you?" My low whisper somehow seemed louder than a shout.

He swallowed hard, still looking at Winter, and she squeezed his side and nodded once. His eyes met mine then, and I was shocked to see that they looked glassy.

Then he spoke one word, so soft that I could barely hear him.

"*Yes.*"

Unable to hold my gaze, he hung his head. "We didn't know about Christine's involvement."

Anger flared, hot and sudden. I rarely lost my temper, but now, I was seeing red. I turned to Winter, clenching my jaw so hard that my teeth ached. "*You* knew? You knew as well? And no one fucking thought to tell me?" My voice rose as I focused on Caiden again, not caring about his stricken gaze. I needed answers, and I was going to get them. Right. Fucking. Now. "You and Dad told me she'd died of a brain haemorrhage!"

"We were going to tell you. I'd already spoken to Dad about it, and we'd agreed to speak to you."

I wasn't interested in Caiden's excuses. "When? *When*? You've had fucking months, *years* to tell me, and you just let me think that her death had been an accident!"

He gaped at me, seemingly lost for words.

My eyes filled with hot, bitter tears, and I blinked hard, refusing to let them fall. "Why? I had every fucking right to know!"

"We—" Caiden swallowed hard. "We were trying to protect you."

"Protect me? By lying? I'm not some fragile fucking child," I roared. "You don't get to make those decisions. She was my mum, too! Don't you think I had the right to know the truth?"

I took in the anguish on my brother's face through a haze of anger. My voice dropped to a raw whisper. "I can't even fucking look at you right now."

Cassius stepped closer, placing his hand on my arm. As I took in the guilt written all over his face, my stomach flipped. "You knew, too?"

He nodded, biting his lip.

"Who else?" My shout seemed to echo through the silent kitchen. "Who fucking else?"

"Zayde," Caiden whispered.

"So everyone..." This time, I didn't even bother to disguise the raw pain in my voice. "So everyone closest to me, everyone that I thought I could trust, has been keeping secrets and lying to me." Pushing away from the counter, I stumbled towards the door. "I need to get out of here."

"You've been drinking." Lena suddenly appeared in the doorway. "You can't go anywhere."

"Did you know?" I almost didn't want to ask the question. Breathing hard through the stinging waves of betrayal that were assaulting me, I stared into her blue eyes, trying to decipher her unreadable gaze. Her eyes flicked from mine to the kitchen, then back again.

"I didn't know until..." She waved a hand towards my former friends, who remained silent behind me.

I released a heavy breath. "Have you been drinking?"

"No."

"Can you get us out of here?"

She bit her lip, glancing to the others again, before she met my gaze. "I'll have to drive your car."

"I don't care." The fucking tears were pricking at my eyes again. "I just need to get out of here. Please."

"Okay."

10

lena

Gripping the steering wheel tightly, I navigated towards my house, unsure where else to go. This was a shitshow. Last night, I'd run away because he was drunk, and honestly, I'd been scared. Scared of my reaction to Weston. Scared of what might happen. Now, though, he was here next to me; he'd been drinking again, and I couldn't run this time.

His silent presence was almost overwhelming. I'd made a huge mistake, and I wasn't sure if he was going to forgive me when I told him the truth. I couldn't tell him now, though—not while he was so worked up.

He needed someone in his corner, and that person was going to be me.

After carefully parking his car in the garage, I got out and headed around to Weston's side. He remained slumped in his seat, eyes closed.

I sighed and tapped on the window. His eyes flew open, and a smile curved over his lips. Ignoring the butterflies, which I was a master at, I opened his door. The smile fell from his face, replaced by sadness and pain as he remembered what had happened.

"Why are we here?" He climbed out of the car, stretching, and I definitely didn't notice the way his muscles flexed. No, I was immune to Weston's charms.

"I didn't know where else to go. You need to get some rest."

He nodded. "Okay," he said softly. I'd never seen him so subdued, and another rush of guilt suffocated me.

This was my fault.

I led him through the house to the bedrooms. My parents were on a different level to me, thankfully, because I really didn't want to have to explain why Weston was here so late in the evening, drunk, without Cassius.

Stopping outside the door to the guest room that he normally used when he stayed over, I turned to him. "Get some rest. You'll feel better if you sleep it off."

"Will you stay?" He stared at me from beneath his thick lashes, his eyes imploring me. "Just for a bit. I don't...I don't wanna be alone."

"Okay. Just for a bit, then. My parents will kill me, and probably you, if they find us together."

He gave me a half-smile at that as he stepped into the room and kicked off his trainers. "Nah, your parents love me."

Pulling off my own boots, I glanced around the room, deciding I'd hang out on the sofa. It converted into a bed, but since I wasn't planning on staying long, there was no point converting it. "Blinds down?" I waved my hand towards the floor-to-ceiling windows that showcased the view over the ocean. Our house was built into the cliffs, and most rooms looked out over the horizon.

"Not yet. Come here?"

I looked up to find him lying on his back on the huge bed, watching me through heavy-lidded eyes. How was I supposed to resist him? My defences couldn't handle the full force of his attention.

Instead of replying, I moved towards the bed. It was probably a bad idea, but I'd just stay as far from him as possible. The bed was massive; it would be easy enough to keep my distance.

He seemed to have other ideas. As I reached the bed, he sat up and tugged me so I fell into him, then wrapped his arm around my shoulders.

Stiffening, I went to pull away, but I was stopped by his voice, cracked and broken.

"I need you."

My flimsy defences melted away, and I let my body curl into his, tentatively laying my arm across his chest. So many feelings were overwhelming me—need, want, guilt, and underneath it all, the dread that I couldn't seem to shake, no matter how much I told myself that I could trust Weston. That fear stopped me from getting close.

"Thank you," he murmured, and I felt a whisper of a kiss on the top of my head as my eyes closed.

The next thing I knew, my eyes were flying open at the sound of my mum's voice, hissing somewhere close to my ear.

"Lena Damaris Drummond!"

I became aware that I was lying in pretty much the same position I'd fallen asleep in—head buried in Weston's shoulder, one arm slung across his body, and his arm wrapped around me. We were on top of the covers, fully clothed, but I knew I had some explaining to do.

Weston was somehow still asleep. Lifting my head, I carefully dislodged his arm and slipped away from his body, before turning to face my mum with a finger to my lips.

She frowned at me but remained silent as she followed me out into the hallway, where I closed the door behind us. I walked far enough down the hallway that Weston wouldn't hear us if he woke up, then stopped.

"Go on, then." She raised her brows expectantly.

"What?"

"Explain to me what I walked into this morning." Folding her arms, she leaned against the wall. There was humour in her gaze, and I relaxed slightly. If my dad had been the one to find us...yeah, I would've been a lot less relaxed.

"It's not my story to tell," I began. "But West has fallen out with the others. Like, properly fallen out with them. He-he was really upset and he wanted to get away and I didn't know what to do," I finished in a rush.

My mum's expression morphed into one of concern. "Oh no. I'll call Arlo?" She phrased it like a question, and I shook my head.

"No. Um. Arlo's involved in it, kind of, so I don't think it's a good idea."

"Right. In that case, let's get some breakfast ready. I take it Weston had been drinking last night?" She knew about the party. Lucky for me, she was pretty chill about everything. Both my parents were, in general.

"Yes. I didn't drink, though. Also, nothing happened with..." I trailed off, my cheeks heating, making my mum laugh.

"Oh, Lena. I know. You were both fully clothed on top of the bed." Strolling off down the hallway, she tossed over her shoulder, "He'd make a wonderful son-in-law, by the way."

"Mum, please." I groaned.

"Just saying." She smiled innocently as I caught up with her at the bottom of the stairs that led to the upper floor, and I rolled my eyes, choosing not to respond. I needed to end this conversation. Now.

"Give me ten mins? I want to have a shower and change." Without waiting for an answer, I began backing away from her, heading in the direction of my bedroom. She smirked at me, before making her way up the stairs.

"What do you think your boyfriend would like for breakfast?" she asked from the open fridge as I rejoined her in the kitchen after my shower. We normally had staff who prepared food, but at the weekends my parents liked to do their own thing.

"Mum!"

"Okay, okay. I won't say another word." She mimed zipping her lips shut, causing me to roll my eyes yet again.

"Let's do a fry-up," I decided. "Do we have all the stuff?"

"Avocado on toast? With poached eggs?" she countered.

"If you want to make that, why are you asking me?"

"I'm only teasing you. I know Weston would rather have a fried breakfast." Pulling a carton of eggs out of the fridge, she smiled at me. "I'll do the eggs, you do the mushrooms."

We worked in silence, preparing the food. My dad wandered in when it was almost ready. "Mmm, something smells good." He placed a kiss on the top of my mum's head, before heading over to me and doing the same. "Four plates?"

"Yes. West's here."

He raised a brow at me. "Without Cassius?"

I nodded. "Yeah. They've had a falling-out, so please be nice."

Tutting, he began setting out the pile of plates around the table. "Me? I'm always nice."

"Hmmm. Just...be tactful, okay?"

"I am the epitome of discretion, I'll have you know." He waltzed off to the coffee machine and turned it on.

"Okay, but please don't mention Cass to him. Or Zayde. Or Caiden. Oh, Winter, too."

He laughed, clearly not taking me seriously enough. "Anyone else?"

"His dad. Actually, it might be better if you just don't talk at all."

"Sure. Would you like—" His sarcastic words came to an abrupt halt as Weston came in, barefoot and rubbing his eyes. All tousled hair and sleepy, in his faded jeans and grey T-shirt, he looked gorgeous. Then, I took in the sadness in his eyes, and my mouth turned down.

My mum, intuitive as ever, took the initiative. "Morning, West. Take a seat at the table. Breakfast is ready."

He slid into a seat, and I took the one across from him. We were mostly silent as we all ate, my dad trying to lighten the mood by drawing Weston into a conversation about cars. Weston replied in monosyllables, and I spent the entire time pushing my food around my plate, my appetite gone as the guilt gnawed at my insides.

I thought I'd been doing the right thing. But I hadn't. I'd hurt the boy I loved irreparably.

And if he found out the part I'd played, he might never forgive me.

11

weston

My entire world had gone dark.

Cade, Cass, and my dad were blowing up my phone, but I ignored their calls and messages. My initial anger had turned to numbness, but every now and then, the stabbing pain would rage through me. Losing my mum when I was only thirteen had left a huge hole in my life, and the thought that my family and closest friends had been keeping a secret from me had really fucking hurt.

The day passed in a blur, Lena a constant presence yet giving me my own space. After she'd dragged me into the media room, that was. I zoned out, watching mindless action movies while she curled up in a chair off to the side of the room, working on her laptop. I couldn't even remember what I ate; everything was bland and tasteless.

That night, sleep finally pulled me under sometime around 4:00 a.m., and I woke late in the morning, with the sun high in the sky.

I knew where I wanted to go.

Palming my keys in my hand, I pushed down on the latch of the wrought iron gate that led into the small hilltop cemetery. I made my way up the familiar winding path and picked my way across to the black marble headstone that marked my mum's resting place.

Joanne Cavendish. Beloved wife and mother.

Suicide. Could I have seen the warning signs? Was there anything else I could have done?

Sinking to the ground, I leaned my head against the cool marble. "I'm sorry, Mum. Sorry I failed you. I wish I'd known. I wish...I wish things could have been different. I wish I could've helped you."

By the time I'd finished speaking, my throat was raw and my eyes were stinging, swollen from the tears I'd finally given in to.

Blowing out a heavy breath, I pulled my phone from my pocket and sent a text to the one person that I knew would be there for me, the person who understood my situation and hadn't let me down.

Me: I need you to make me forget.

When the reply came, the relief was instant.

Come to me.

The Drummond home was silent as I entered the foyer, using the key Lena had given me. I headed into the huge open lounge area, and there she was. Silhouetted against a wall of glass, the sun setting over the sea behind her, she looked...

She'd dressed down in loose black cotton trousers and a black vest top, and her ever-permanent black eye makeup was absent. As I approached her, she held up a bag, the sound of bottles clinking inside. She eyed me cautiously for a moment, before dropping her gaze, licking her lips.

Nervous. Lena was nervous?

"Want to get drunk and high?"

All I could do was nod. Although she wasn't looking at me, she turned on her heel and headed for the doors that led out to one of the outside areas. All white stone, looking out over the sea, there was a firepit and a covered area with huge outdoor cube-shaped sofas, big enough to lie on.

She paused in the doorway. "Wait. I got your stuff. It's in the guest room."

"Thanks." I'd asked her if she could persuade Cassius to bring me some of my clothes while I was at the cemetery. "I'll grab a shower and change, then meet you out here?"

When I returned, feeling more human, Lena was curled up on one of the sofas, stretching out her legs in front of her. Glancing up at me, she patted the space next to her. Kicking off my shoes, I crawled onto the sofa and reclined back, propped up by the cushions behind me.

"West?" Her voice was low and hesitant.

I took a deep breath. "I don't want to talk. I want to forget."

"Okay."

Fuck knows how much time had passed, but by the time I was feeling numb, the sky was completely dark, dotted with stars, and the only light came from the firepit and the dim glow of the lights that were inlaid into the floor, illuminating the walkways.

Finishing up the last of the joint I'd been sharing with Lena, I flicked the stub away and rolled onto my side, almost completely horizontal by this point. The alcohol and weed had left me with no fucking filter, because when I opened my mouth, what came out was "Why is it weird between us lately?"

Lena stared at me, her mouth opening and closing for a moment, before she turned back to stare up at the sky. "I don't know."

Propping myself up on my elbow, I reached out and ran a finger down her arm, watching with satisfaction as goosebumps pebbled along her skin.

Fuck. I shouldn't be touching her. But I didn't want to stop. "I do. I think you like me."

Her breath hitched, and she squeezed her eyes shut.

My dick stirred, and I shifted my position. As much as the drinks and the weed had lowered my inhibitions around her, something was telling me that I needed to take it slow with this girl.

But, *fuck*.

We might never get this chance again.

"I wanted to kiss you on Friday night at the party." I admitted the truth that I hadn't even been able to admit to myself at the time. "Did you want me to kiss you?"

She remained silent as I let my finger trail up her arm again and onto her collarbone. Her chest rose and fell, her breath coming faster. "You're so responsive," I murmured, as my finger continued to journey across her collarbone, up her neck, and finally to her lips.

A tiny whimper escaped her as I traced the outline of

her lips. "Guess what?" I leaned closer, my breath skating across her skin. I waited until her eyelids fluttered open again and she met my gaze. "I know I probably shouldn't, but I really want to kiss you right now."

A soft gasp escaped her lips; then they parted slightly, and her tongue darted out to touch the tip of my finger.

That was the only sign I needed. My hand moved to cup her jaw. "I need...I want to forget."

I could feel her soft tremble, but she inclined her head towards me, and I slanted my mouth over hers. She melted beneath me as I explored her mouth, touching, teasing, tasting. Her hand slid up around the back of my neck, holding me in place as her body shivered against mine.

Fuck. She tasted so good.

Through the haze of alcohol and weed, my brain reminded me that this wasn't a good idea. Drunk, high, confused, and all the other fucked-up emotions I'd been experiencing—I didn't need to drag Lena into my shit. Not to mention, Cass would kill me. If I ever spoke to him again.

With an effort, I drew back, leaving her lying there staring up at me with wide eyes, her lips wet and swollen. She sucked in a shaky breath, then cleared her throat. "Uh."

I waited, but it didn't seem like she was planning on saying anything else. "Wanna watch something?" I suggested, when the silence became uncomfortable.

"Yeah." Her mouth curved up into a half-smile, and before I knew what I was doing, I found myself pressing a kiss to the corner of her mouth. Straightening up, I grinned down at her as she rubbed her hand across her face, gathering herself.

We stumbled back inside, not drunk but both of us buzzed enough that our progress was unsteady. She began heading in the direction of the media room, but I caught her arm, tugging her back against my chest. "Your room." I didn't miss her shiver at my low command, and I smiled again, loving the way her body fit perfectly against mine, her reaction to me heady and intoxicating.

Of course, Lena being Lena, she pulled away from me. I could almost see her shields dropping back into place as she took off down the stairs towards her bedroom.

When I crashed through her doorway, steadying myself on the frame, she was hitting the keyboard that stood in front of the huge monitor on her desk. I didn't even look at the screen. My brain had shut down, and all I wanted was to feel her body against me again. Stalking up behind her, I gripped her around her waist, pulling her into my chest, and threw us both back on the bed.

"Wait!" The urgency in Lena's tone made me pause.

"What's wrong?"

Her eyes flicked between me and her desk, and then she composed herself. "Nothing. What do you want to watch?"

"Whatever you want."

"What about that new series about serial killers?"

I took in the expression on her face and raised a brow. "Serial killers, huh?"

She nodded. "Yep."

With a shrug, I settled back against her headboard. "Yeah, okay. Sounds good."

***

Hours later, I woke, my eyes gritty and my mouth dry. Dragging my phone from my pocket, I squinted at the screen. Four forty-two in the morning. The room was dark, but I could dimly make out Lena curled up on the far side of her bed, away from me. Careful not to disturb her, I moved off the bed and headed into her bathroom, where I downed a glass of water and helped myself to her mouthwash.

Feeling more human, I returned to her bedroom, leaving the bathroom light on and the door ajar so I could see what I was doing. My keys had been digging into my leg, left in my pocket for however many hours I'd been lying there, so I fished them out and placed them on Lena's desk, as soundlessly as I could. As I slid my hand away, I knocked Lena's computer mouse, waking up the screen. The TV app was still open, scrolling through the menu showing the latest available series.

I hit the button to close out of the app, and at the same time, a blinking message alert in the corner of the screen caught my eye.

A very familiar message alert.

What the fuck? Clicking on the icon, I was faced with a login screen I knew all too well.

Wait.

The pieces fell into place.

Striding over to the bed, I flicked on the bedside lamp, then shook Lena's shoulder, gritting my teeth. There had to be an explanation for this.

Her eyes flew open, and as she took in the expression on my face, hers paled. "What's happened?"

"You've got some explaining to do, Lena." I took a harsh breath. "Or should I call you *Mercury*?"

12

lena

This couldn't be happening. It was a dream. No, not a dream. A nightmare. But as I stared up at Weston, watching his face torn between anger and pleading, I knew I had to come clean.

Blinking the sleep from my eyes, I cleared my throat, pulling myself into a seated position.

"What are you talking about?" My voice was shaky.

"Don't insult my intelligence. I saw your computer. I saw the login screen and the message alert."

His eyes pleaded with me to deny what he was saying, to come up with any explanation that would mean he was wrong.

"Okay." He was making me nervous, looming over the bed. Why did he affect me this way? "Can you sit down?" I figured it was best to go with full honesty. "You're...you're making me nervous."

He frowned but took a seat on the bed, his eyes never leaving mine.

"You're right," I said quietly, then spoke the words that I

knew would change things irreversibly between us. "I'm Mercury. And I know you're Nitro."

The room fell deadly silent.

His jaw worked, his expressive eyes flitting through a whirlwind of emotions, before he closed them.

When he opened his eyes again, my heart fractured as I watched him shut down. It was like the last bit of light in him had been extinguished. His eyes were dead, his expression blank.

"Please explain," he said tonelessly, and tears filled my eyes.

"West." I reached for him, my hand shaking.

"*No.*"

I pulled my hand back as if it was on fire. "I-I'm Mercury, yes. I didn't know that you were Nitro until...until some of the stuff you asked me to look into proved to me who you were. Everything that was happening with Winter, you know?"

"Why didn't you say anything?" he asked in the same toneless voice.

"How could I? You know we're not allowed to compromise our identity."

A bitter laugh fell from his mouth. "You were already compromised when you found out who I was. You've had *months* to come clean."

I opened my mouth to speak, but he wasn't finished. "And you. *You* were the one who fucked up everything with my family."

My jaw dropped, and I welcomed the thread of anger that burned through me. "Wait a minute. I sent you that video because I thought you had a right to know the truth about your mum. I hadn't...I haven't had it for long, otherwise I would have sent it sooner. You deserved to know. Can't—"

He held up his hand, stopping me in my tracks. "Another thing you lied to me about. When I asked you if you knew what had happened, you said you'd just found out."

"I had! Okay, not long before that, but I couldn't exactly tell you I was Mercury, could I?" Leaning forwards on the bed, I pinned him with a savage look, and he bared his teeth at me.

"Why? Why, Lena? Why did you have to be Mercury?" His voice grew louder. "You were the one person left that I thought hadn't hid things from me. Do you know how fucking betrayed I feel right now?"

"Because—"

"Why!"

I shoved at his chest, the words ripping from my throat. "*Because I've been in—I've liked you for fucking years*!"

"What?"

His face was no longer blank, and confusion filled his eyes.

"Um." I buried my face in my hands, my anger gone, replaced with embarrassment. This was officially the worst day of my life. "I liked you when we were kids. You know," I mumbled. "I *liked*, liked you. You were into computers, so I got into them. And-and I realised I was really good at what I was doing."

Tentatively, I raised my head. He paced next to the bed, his eyes wild. "I can't fucking deal with this right now. You—" A frustrated growl tore from his throat. "I don't even know what that has to do with all this. You tell me you liked me, but you hid who you were from me. I *trusted* you. As Mercury, there was so much shit we dealt with together. You know more than my brother does about some things. And yet, whenever I saw you in person, you acted like I was irrelevant to you. Like you didn't—" He broke off, clenching his fists, before he spun to face me. "What the fuck, Lena? That's fucked up."

"I was trying to protect myself," I said lamely, unable to explain. My head was spinning, trying to articulate what I couldn't put into words. My lip trembled, and I grasped at my bedcovers, trying to ground myself. "I wanted you. I wanted you so much, but I couldn't...we couldn't..."

His eyes darkened, all the anger that had built up inside him aimed in my direction. At that moment, I barely even recognised him. This wasn't the Weston I knew. It was like my secret was the final straw, and now he was lost, irrational and wild, and I was caught in the eye of the storm.

"You wanted me? Really? Is this what you fucking wanted?" He pounced, pinning me beneath his body. Grabbing my hands, he held me down effortlessly, and all of my years of martial arts and self-defence training went out the window at the words he'd used, spoken in that tone, and the way his weight pinned me down.

I. Couldn't. Breathe.

My entire body froze, paralysed under him. "Get off me! Get off!" My words were strangled, barely making it through my throat, which was closing up. Tears poured down my cheeks unchecked, and he jerked backwards in shock, immediately releasing his grip on my body, putting some much-needed distance between us. The anger immediately disappeared from his eyes, and instead, his wide-eyed, alarmed gaze fixated on me in horror.

"Lena, I would *never*—"

"No! Please... Please go." My words were almost incomprehensible through my sobs, as the memories I'd been able to suppress for years flooded back. "*Please*," I managed between sobs, and finally, he moved, the door slamming behind him as he left me alone.

I felt like crawling out of my own skin. The only thought on my mind was to get to the beach, my one place of refuge. Somehow, I made it through the house, to the outside lift that moved up and down the cliff face, and descended to the tiny, sheltered beach where my family's boat was moored at a small wooden jetty.

Collapsing down onto the pebbles, blissfully alone, I leaned back against the rough stone of the cliff and buried my face in my arms. My body shook with anger at myself for my reaction after all this time, my mind battered by a graphic flashback of the trauma I'd thought I'd overcome.

I let myself fall apart.

13

lena

AGE FOURTEEN

I was on top of the world. I'd scored an invite to Niall's house party, thanks to my skateboarder friend Jax. Niall was one of the hottest boys at Highnam Academy, Alstone High's rival school. I wasn't interested in him in that way, but the kids at Highnam Academy were far less stuck-up than the ones at my own school.

The party was everything I hoped for. No adults, plenty of alcohol, and maybe, just maybe, a boy I could practise kissing on. My heart belonged to Weston Cavendish, but I knew he only saw me as Cassius' little sister. After tonight, though, things would be different. I'd prove to him that I was girlfriend material.

Jax had disappeared off, but I was having a great time dancing and drinking, the alcohol buzzing through my veins, just enough to make me feel comfortable. Over in the corner of the room, I saw a boy with wavy dark brown hair leaning against the wall. Probably about my brother's age, maybe even a little older, he had on faded jeans and a dark blue T-shirt with some kind of round logo on it in red. When he caught my eye, he smiled and pushed off the wall, heading towards me.

As he approached, I wiped my palms on my leggings, suddenly nervous and second-guessing my decision. Should I save my first kiss for Weston?

It only took me a couple of seconds to make up my mind. He'd kissed plenty of girls, and I needed to wow him.

"I saw you checking me out." The mystery boy smiled again when he got to me. His whole vibe was unthreatening, and he sort of reminded me of Harry Styles, so I relaxed and called on my sparse acting skills to play it cool.

"I saw *you* checking *me* out, actually."

He laughed at that, taking another step closer. "You're funny. What's your name? I haven't seen you around here before."

"Imogen. And I'm not from around here." I borrowed the name of one of my classmates, knowing that even though it was clear he didn't know who I was, he was likely to be aware of my dad's name and might put two and two together.

"Nice to meet you. The name's Bobby." Without pausing for breath, he continued. "Now we've got the introductions out of the way, why don't we go somewhere quieter?"

In reply, I inclined my head, and he took my hand, leading me out of the lounge and into the back of the house. He kept going, through the tiny, crowded kitchen, and out of the back door into the outside space. The houses here were all terraced, with tiny, paved yards and gates leading into an alley that ran along the back of all of the houses in the street.

Glancing around the yard, which was mostly full of

people talking and smoking, he paused for a minute, then headed in the direction of the gate. Sliding the lock to open it, he eased down the latch.

If I'd been paying more attention to my surroundings rather than focusing on the fact that I was about to kiss a boy for the first time, I might have thought the way he inclined his head at the guy standing in a shadowy corner of the yard was a little strange. Then again, I might not. I couldn't torture myself with the what-ifs.

Out in the cold, dark alley, he gripped my arm lightly. "Come on, sweetheart. This way." He tugged me towards the far end of the alley, which was essentially a dead end at that point in time since it led to one of the entrances to a park, and the gates were locked at dusk every day.

"I-I don't know." I hesitated, stopping dead.

Behind me, there was the sound of a pebble being kicked.

Dread crawled up my spine.

I turned slowly, as Bobby's grip on my arm tightened.

A shadowy figure stepped forwards.

What happened next came in flashes. A hand over my mouth. The noises of the party, still loud in the alley, muffling my cries. Calloused, dirty fingernails. An arm around my throat. Falling to the floor, with a body pressing me down, sneering, "Is this what you fucking wanted?" The cold, grimy cobbles beneath me. My futile struggles, followed by numbness.

Dimly, I registered the sound of shouting, and the pressure on my body was suddenly gone.

"Fuck." The voices sounded close to my ear as I drifted in and out of conscious thought.

Blackness descended, sudden and blissful.

The rest of the night and following day was a blur. I remembered a kind female doctor speaking to me, carefully helping me to lie on my bed back at home, which for some reason smelled of antiseptic, paper crinkling under me as I lay down. My mum, bursting into tears and hugging me tightly to her like she'd never let me go. Scrubbing my body in the shower over and over again until my skin was raw and dotted with pinpricks of blood.

No matter how hard I scrubbed, no matter how raw my skin was, I still felt dirty. Tainted. Unclean.

In the aftermath, I built up a picture. Lying on my bed two days after everything had happened, my mum told me all that she knew as she stroked through my hair with familiar, comforting movements. Every now and then, she'd glance down at my thighs and catch her breath at the finger-shaped bruises there.

There had been two guys. They'd been stopped mid-assault by the arrival of James Granville and his cousin, Tim Hyde. Our families had a bit of a rivalry going on, but at that moment, I'd never been more grateful for them. As they approached, the guys had run away, and although Tim had given chase, he was unable to catch them. James had carried me to his car and driven me home, where my mum had been alone as my dad and Cassius were away on a father/son bonding experience.

Young, scared, and alone, it was a relief to let my mum deal with the burden. Estella Drummond may have been small in stature, but she was a tigress when it came to defending her family.

"Never underestimate a Drummond woman." On the third day following the assault, she swept into my room, with her version of armour on, aka a tight dress, impossibly high heels, and immaculate hair and makeup, her features set in a severe look. "I know you've been adamant about keeping this quiet, so as not to affect our family name, but we're not letting this go. I've spoken to a friend, and these…" She paused, her voice wobbling slightly before she took a deep breath. "These animals won't be bothering anyone again."

Relief swept through my entire body, and I began to shake. My mum crossed the room to me and pulled me into her arms as we both cried together.

Afterwards, I begged her not to tell Cassius or my dad. The guilt and shame overwhelmed me, threatening to pull me under. Logically, I knew I had nothing to feel ashamed of.

But I couldn't make it stop.

14

lena

T his was it. I let my tears cleanse my body, allowing myself to finally let go. I had a fucking amazing therapist who had worked through the assault with me, but there had always been something inside me. Something I hadn't allowed myself to let go of. I'd built a shell, and now the rawness was exposed to the open, it was cathartic.

"Lena?" A small hand touched my arm gently, and I raised my head, blinking my swollen eyes. Winter's face came into focus.

"What are you doing here?" My voice was a hoarse croak, and I wasn't even sure if she understood what I was saying.

"West." She tugged my arm gently. "Come on, let's get you inside. You're shivering."

Huh. I was, and I hadn't even noticed. As she helped me to my feet, I turned, and the next second I was being enveloped in warm, strong arms.

"Fuck, sis. What's going on?" My brother kissed the top of my head.

"I don't want to talk—" I started to say, then realised that actually, that wasn't true. I *did* want to talk about it. To finally purge my mind and body of this secret shame that had left me unable and unwilling to develop any kind of meaningful relationship with Weston. "Can we go inside? I'll tell you then." My arms slipped around Cassius' waist, and I felt him sigh.

"Course we can. Come on."

Curled up on the huge L-shaped sofa in front of the floor-to-ceiling windows, a fluffy blanket wrapped around my shoulders, I sipped the hot chocolate Winter had made for me, while I tried to work out where to begin.

"I only want to talk about this once," I began. "So please don't-don't interrupt me, okay? Because I might not be able to get it all out." From her position beside me, Winter nodded and squeezed my arm reassuringly. Holding my breath, I flicked my gaze to my brother's, where he sat across from me on the L of the sofa, his expression unreadable. He also nodded, and I let out my breath in relief. "Okay. Thank you. It happened when I was fourteen, when you and Dad went on that outdoor skills week away..."

As I spoke, relaying what had happened, I felt Winter's soft gasp next to me, and she inched closer, putting her arm around my shoulders. I allowed my head to lean against her, feeling so tired all of a sudden. So drained. Cassius... His whole body was practically vibrating with tension, his fists and jaw clenched so tightly that I knew he was going to explode the second I stopped speaking.

Leaning forwards, I placed my hand on his knee. "Mum dealt with the guys. I wasn't—I didn't want it to damage our reputation, so I didn't want to go to the police."

"Fuck that!" He stared at me, breathing hard. "Fucking

fuck the reputation. You were attacked, Lena! People need to pay."

"Would you have really wanted the scandal? Would Dad? To have our name dragged through the courts, to be the focus of gossip, for it to be my word against theirs?" I was crying again now, and I was shocked to see tears in my brother's eyes, too.

"But—" He cut himself off, burying his face in his hands. When his shoulders shook, I lunged forwards and threw myself at him.

"Cass, please."

"Fuck, Lena. I just can't...I want to *kill* the people that did this to you."

"Mum sorted it. Believe me, they're never going to hurt anyone again."

Raising his head, he stared at me. "*Our* mum? Estella Drummond? Tiny woman who looks like she wouldn't hurt a fly?"

A laugh burst out of me unexpectedly, and his lips curved up in response.

"Yeah. She— She's friends with, um, someone. Someone who can make things...and people...disappear."

Winter's voice came from behind me. "Why do all of you know people with all these connections? It's not normal."

I turned to her, smiling. "We're Drummonds."

She rolled her eyes but returned my smile.

"Were you targeted because of who you were?" Cassius hugged me closer, swiping my hair away from my face so he could look into my eyes.

"No. It was a random, unprovoked attack. I guess they thought I was an easy target or whatever." I laughed, although I didn't find any humour in it. "Too bad for them that I'm a Drummond."

We were silent for a moment, Winter and Cassius digesting everything I'd told them. My eyes met Winter's, and I took a deep breath, immediately feeling lighter as I said the words. "You can tell Cade, by the way. And Zayde, too, I guess. I don't want to talk about it again."

"West?" She prodded gently, before her face fell. "Although he's not exactly talking to any of us at the moment."

"No." Shaking my head firmly, I looked between them both. "I need to tell him. I owe him an explanation."

An expression of horror suddenly crossed her face. "Shit. You know what this means, right?" Throwing her head back against the sofa, she let out a huge groan. "I'm going to have to tell Cade that James played the hero again."

Cassius laughed loudly as the tension in the room dissipated. "This should be good."

Winter raised a sceptical brow. "It really won't. You know how much he dislikes James."

"I think he secretly likes him."

"Hmm," she said, clearly unconvinced, before she turned serious again. "I hate that you've had to keep this all inside you for so long."

I shrugged, feeling lighter than I had in a very long time. "Yeah, well. Mum knew, obviously, and I had an amazing therapist who helped me to work through everything. But I didn't want to talk about it. At first I felt shame—"

"You have nothing to feel ashamed of. Those sick fucks are nothing but animals." Cassius cut me off angrily, and I hugged him again, trying to calm him.

"I know. I know I don't. I'm just explaining that to begin

with I felt guilt, and shame, and Kaylie, that's my therapist, helped me to work through it all. That's why I started the martial arts classes, too, so that I could always fight my way out of a situation. Anyway. I thought I'd put it all behind me, until now."

Winter glanced at Cassius, then studied me intently. "Cass, can you give me a minute with Lena, alone? Please."

He met her eyes over the top of my head, then nodded, releasing me. "Course. Shout for me when you're done."

When we were alone, Winter spoke softly, her eyes never leaving mine.

"Tell me to bugger off if you don't want to talk about it, but...did something trigger it?"

"West." His name fell from my lips as a sigh, and she nodded.

"I assumed so. You know, he's refused to take any of our calls or reply to our messages, yet today he called me, pretty much ordering me to drop everything and come to you. Do you want to talk about what happened?"

Might as well. She already knew the rest of it. "It was something he said. It was the exact same words that—" I swallowed hard.

"I get it." She squeezed my arm.

"Yeah, and at the time he had me pinned on the bed—" Winter raised a brow at that. "—and it just, I don't know, triggered the memory, and I panicked. I owe him a huge apology. All of you, in fact."

"Wait, *what*? You don't owe anyone anything. You went through something that no one should have to experience, and no one has any right to tell you how you should or shouldn't react."

"No, I'm actually not talking about that." I took a deep breath. "Cass?" I called out, and he immediately re-entered the room, crossing over to us and taking a seat next to me again. "I have something I need to tell you both."

Steeling myself, I let the words fall from my mouth.

"I'm Mercury."

Complete and utter silence.

Then—

"What?"

"Not only that," I continued before Cassius could say anything else, "I sent Weston the footage from the docks. That's how he found out about his mum."

"Oh, fuck." Winter's anguished tone cut through the room. "Okay, let me think about this for a minute. Forgetting the whole secret-identity thing, because I don't think we need to go into that right now, what with everything else that's happened."

Cassius sat forwards on the sofa, shooting me a hard look. Or trying to, at least, although his eyes were still soft with concern. "Yeah, I won't be forgetting that one."

"Didn't think so," I muttered.

"Firstly, it wasn't your fault, so don't feel like you should apologise. The docks footage thing. We should've told him sooner. I've been saying that to Cade for ages, and he...well, I know he'd planned with Arlo to tell West."

"Too late, now," I said sadly.

"How did he react when you told him?"

"About as well as you'd expect. One more secret exposed, one more person that's betrayed him."

"This is such a mess." Winter pinched her brow. "Okay, I need to find him. I don't want him to be alone in this state." She pulled her phone from the small bag that rested by her feet, tapping at the screen. "He's got his location turned off. I can't find him."

A small smile tugged at my lips. "It's a good thing you

have Mercury here. Give me a few, and I'll get you his exact location."

She sat back, looking relieved. "While you do that, I'll call Cade to pick me up. I'm guessing you want to stay here, Cass?"

She guessed correctly. "Yeah. I think we have some stuff to talk about, don't we?" My brother looked at me, his eyes full of emotion, and I nodded.

"We do."

15

weston

B lissfully numb. At last. Eyes closed, I let the room spin as the bottle fell from my grasp. I couldn't smoke here, but I was well on my way to emptying out the hotel minibar. My phone was off, and the drone of the TV distracted me from my thoughts. I wasn't stupid enough to think that no one would find me here, but I knew that the hotel's strict security should at least stop them from getting to my room.

The hotel phone blared loudly, disrupting my peace. Gritting my teeth, I fumbled for the handset, barking out a "What?" into the speaker.

"Excuse me, sir." The voice at the other end was completely unfazed by my rudeness. "I have a Miss Huntington here at the front desk, asking to speak with you. Would you like me to send her up?"

I froze. "No. Fuck, no. I don't want to see anyone."

"Very good, sir. Would you like me to relay a message?"

"No." With that, I replaced the handset in its cradle with a crash and flopped back on the bed.

My eyes flew open at the click of my door unlocking, and I bolted upright.

"West!" Winter flung herself across the room and onto the bed. "I'm sorry, I'm so sorry." Her voice cracked.

My arms went around her automatically, but I held myself tense, in fight-or-flight mode as I met the eyes of two people over her shoulder. Two people that I definitely wasn't ready to face yet.

My dad and my brother.

"Get. Out."

"No." Caiden folded his arms, staring at me challengingly. "Not until you hear what we have to say."

I'd seen that look on my brother's face many times over the years, and because I knew what a stubborn bastard he was, I capitulated with a growl. "Fine. Say what you came here to say, then leave me alone."

He frowned but didn't argue with me.

"How did you get in here, anyway?"

My dad was the one to reply. "Did you realise you were in a hotel owned by Credence Pope?"

"Creed let you break into my room? Brilliant."

"Technically, we didn't break in. We had a key," my brother oh-so-fucking-helpfully pointed out.

"Whatever. Just tell me what you wanted to say."

Winter shuffled off my lap and rearranged herself cross-legged next to me, as my brother perched himself on the side of my bed and my dad took a seat at the desk chair.

"We were wrong not to tell you about your mother sooner." For the first time since they'd entered the room, my dad's face fell, and I saw the anguish he was trying to hide. "Caiden and I...we'd planned to tell you sooner, and

I'm so sorry that we let you down." He leaned forwards, clasping his hands and pinning me with a look that was so full of pain and remorse that it stunned me. "I failed you. I thought—" His voice faltered, and he cleared his throat before continuing. "I thought that I was doing the right thing. I only hope that you can forgive me."

Caiden took over from Dad, his troubled gaze focused on mine. "I'm so fucking sorry, West."

"Why didn't you tell me sooner? Why didn't you tell me when it happened? Do you have any idea of how much guilt and regret I'm feeling right now?"

"Yes, I do know!" His voice was a shout that echoed through the hotel room. "I do know," he repeated more quietly. "Because I've felt that way ever since it happened. I was trying to protect you, so you wouldn't have to feel the way I did." A glazed expression took over his face, his voice cracking as he continued. "I found her, you know. She was so still. So cold. So..." He buried his face in his hands, and Winter crawled across the bed and into his lap, holding him as he broke all over again.

Fuck.

Some of my anger lessened right then. Rationally, I could see that they'd done it with good intentions, although it still did nothing to temper the betrayal and guilt that was tying my stomach in knots.

"Whether you did it for the right reasons or not, you still really hurt me."

"I'm—" Cade started to say, raising his head to meet my gaze.

"Wait. I'm just...look, I can forgive you. Just give me time, okay? I need time. I need...I need to work things through in my own head. I don't want to say anything that can't be taken back."

I'm proud of you, Winter mouthed, and I felt a small smile tugging at my lips. Out of everyone, I knew I'd find her easiest to forgive. She had a heart of gold, and she'd proven her loyalty to us all time and time again.

"I just wanna say one thing." Caiden glanced at Winter, before he returned his attention to me. "Ever since Winter first found out, she was uncomfortable with keeping this from you. She wanted me to tell you. So, please, blame me, but don't blame her." He turned back to her. "I'm so sorry, baby."

She sniffed, her eyes watery, but gave him a smile. "I forgive you. Your heart was in the right place."

"I forgive you, Winter." The words fell from my mouth, unplanned, but I realised I meant them. Staring between my brother and my dad, I shook my head slowly. "You two —give me time."

My dad nodded. "Whatever you need, West. I don't want this to derail all the progress we've made as a family. But I'll own my mistakes. God knows, I've made enough of them."

I nodded and leaned back against the headboard. "I'd like to be alone now." My eyes closed.

The low murmur of Winter and Caiden's voices sounded, before the door opened and closed softly. I let out a heavy breath.

A throat cleared, and my eyes flew open. Winter stood at the side of the bed, her lip pulled between her teeth and hesitance in her gaze. "I just wanted to say something to you quickly, now the others have gone."

My curiosity was piqued. "What is it?"

"Lena."

At her name, my insides twisted again. "I don't want to speak about her. She—her betrayal hurts the most in a way, because this whole fucking time she's been hiding behind a false identity."

"Yeah, she told me about that." Winter sighed. "But has she, really? Maybe she had her reasons for doing what she did." Gazing out of the window with a faraway expression, she sighed again, before turning back to me. "Please, just go easy on her, okay? She's been through some things. It's not my place to talk about them, and it's up to her whatever she decides to tell you, but please be careful with her."

"I don't know how to feel about all this, and I'm still too angry to be rational," I admitted.

Stepping closer, she leaned over the bed and kissed my cheek. "I know. Just remember, though—she's strong; so strong, but there's a vulnerability to her. All I'm saying is, be careful with her, West."

"Was...is she okay?" I thought back to how she'd completely frozen under me, all the colour draining from her face, and the debilitating terror in her eyes. *Fuck.* I wished more than anything that I could take it all back. I never wanted to see that look in her eyes again.

Winter drew back, giving me a sad smile. "She will be."

We both stared at one another in silence for a moment, before she gave another sigh. "Are you sure you want to be left alone right now?"

"Yeah. I need some time. I'm so tired. Tired of it all."

"Okay." She headed towards the door, then paused. "One more thing. No pressure, and you need to deal with everything in your own time, but just think about sending Cass a text, will you? I've never seen him this down. He's not the Cass we know and love, and I just...I know it's not my place, but think about it, okay?"

The door closed behind her, and I reached for my phone.

Time to face the real world.

Ignoring the notifications that lit up my phone with a frequency I'd never seen before, I navigated straight to my message thread with my best mate.

242 unread messages.

I rolled my eyes, unable to help my smile. Cassius Drummond, dramatic as ever. The smile slipped from my face as I scrolled through his increasingly desperate messages.

Fuck.

How did I respond?

Me: 242 messages, huh?

The three dots showed up immediately, and less than thirty seconds later, I had a reply.

Cass: I was aiming for 250 but I guess I fell short
Cass: Are you ok? I'm so fucking sorry mate
Me: I will be
Cass: Where are you? When are you coming home?
Me: In London in a hotel. Was trying to get away but I guess there was a Cavendish intervention
Cass: Good. Winter said she was coming for you. We're all worried

Guilt burned through me yet again.

Me: I needed time to think
Cass: I get it. See you tomorrow?

Me: I'm not coming back to the house yet. I need a few days
Cass: *gif of a crying man*
Me: *eyeroll emoji* Don't guilt trip me

Then, because I really didn't want to upset him, knowing how he used humour as a defence mechanism sometimes, I sent him another message.

Me: Pool at the Student Union on Weds? 4?
Cass: *grin emoji* Prepare to lose

I sent him the middle finger emoji, and he replied with a gif of a man saying "you're going down."

Guess we were on our way back to normality, then. Yeah, we'd have things to discuss, but our friendship was getting back on track.

Next, I opened up my encrypted Kryptos app that allowed me to send and receive messages to Mercury, Xenon, and Promethium, and bypassing Mercury's traitorous name, hit the notification from Xenon.

Scrolling through the updates, I saw that Xenon's program had flagged up a load of new updates for Martin Smith, the guy I'd been investigating at Alstone Holdings.

Going through the data would have to wait, though. Fuck thinking about anything else right now. Rolling onto my side, I climbed off the bed and headed for the fridge. I had a minibar to get through.

16

lena

A week. A whole week in which Weston hadn't been home. Not that I was checking or anything, but I may have been tracking his phone location.

Two days after everything had blown up between us, I made an emergency appointment with my therapist. We rarely met these days, but she was the one person I trusted to be completely impartial and would give me the space and time to pick apart how I was feeling. I'd built myself up to be untouchable, invincible, and in seconds, it had all come crashing down.

The relief I'd felt when she told me that there was nothing abnormal about the way I'd reacted—not that there was a "normal" way that anyone should be, but I'd panicked, thinking I was losing all the progress I'd made. After the assault, I'd been in a dark place for quite a long time. I'd clawed my way out of it, using therapy and training in martial arts as my light, building up my shields so that I'd never be so helpless again. Martial arts in particular had given me discipline, focus, and I'd finally felt in control once again. Being able to read my opponent and fight back—there was something so empowering about it. I hadn't stuck to just one discipline, either, and I'd acquired a range of skills over the time I'd been practising.

Anyway, after the appointment with my therapist, it was crystal clear to me. I needed to speak to Weston, to try to make him understand why I'd reacted that way to him.

Oh yeah, and I needed to apologise for keeping the whole Mercury thing a secret. One step at a time, though, that's what Kaylie had kept reiterating during our appointment.

Pausing outside the Alstone College Student Union, I smoothed down my top. Outwardly, I looked good—or like myself, at least. Black, loose T-shirt slipping off my shoulders, short black pleated skirt, fishnet tights, chunky boots, and a studded black leather belt I'd looped around and around my arm as a makeshift bracelet.

My phone tracking said Weston was in this building. I knew from my intel that he'd been staying with his friend Rumi, and I was glad he hadn't been alone, but he hadn't been home yet, which concerned me.

I slipped through the doors and headed down the stairs. The first person I saw as I made my way to the bar area was Jessa De Witt. Although, this wasn't the perfectly poised Jessa De Witt I knew. This wasn't the beautiful, rich, and popular girl, best friend to Portia Thompson, the queen bee on campus (or so she liked to think).

This version was a hollowed-out shell of herself. Limp hair, no makeup, dark circles under her eyes. A baggy grey hoodie covered her body, the sleeves pulled down over her hands.

"Jessa?" We'd never been friends, never really spoken, being two years apart in age and due to her dislike and jealousy of Winter, but things had kind of changed since the night at the docks. The Belarusian gang whom Winter's mum was working with had kidnapped her, mistakenly believing her to be Caiden's girlfriend, and from what I'd heard, it had been a traumatic experience for her. I just hadn't realised how badly it had affected her until now. My brother had added me to a group chat with her, Winter, and Kinslee after the whole ordeal, but we'd stuck to light topics—mostly memes, courtesy of Cassius.

She gave me a small smile that didn't reach her eyes and went to move past me. "Oh, hi."

"Wait." I placed my hand on her arm. "Are you..." What could I say that would help? Stepping closer, I lowered my voice, although we were currently alone in the area just outside the bar. "Jessa. Have you spoken to anyone about what happened?"

A dull pain filled her eyes, and she shook her head slowly.

Rummaging in my small bag, I pulled out my therapist's card and pressed it into her hand. "Here. If you ever need to speak to anyone, she really helped me." I nodded towards the card. "You don't have to deal with this alone."

"Thanks," she whispered, clasping the card with shaking fingers. Swallowing hard, she composed herself, then looked at me. "What are you doing here, anyway?"

Both of us were relieved by the change of subject. "I'm looking for Weston. Have you seen him?"

"Yes." Her brows pulled together. "I think...yes. He was on the sofas in the chillout area when I saw him."

"Thanks."

Leaving her outside the bar, I weaved my way through the crowds to the very back of the huge space where groups of sofas were arranged against the wall, packed full of people. My body turned on instinct, the pull of him so strong that it led me to him like a homing beacon.

I sucked in a shocked breath, all the air leaving my lungs as I saw him sprawled on the furthest sofa, next to a couple of girls who thankfully seemed more interested in talking to each other. His glazed eyes were ringed with dark circles. In one hand he gripped a cup, beer sloshing out of the side as he balanced it on the arm of the chair. The other hand rested on the back of the sofa. I watched, suddenly rooted to the spot as a gorgeous girl with wavy blonde hair swung herself into his lap and his arm came down from the back of the sofa to snake around her waist.

Everything happened at once.

Maybe I wasn't thinking straight, but I had unfinished business with Weston Cavendish, and I wasn't about to let another girl fool around with him, not until he'd heard what I'd come to tell him. I stalked over to them, gripping the girl's arms and pulling her from Weston's lap.

Her eyes widened as she took in the expression on my face, and she swallowed nervously.

Releasing my grip, I waited until her eyes met mine, and then I spoke, carefully enunciating every word so there would be no misunderstanding.

"He's off limits."

She stared at me for a moment, before mumbling something about not wanting to be in the middle of drama, then disappeared into the crowds. That dealt with, I turned to Weston.

He stared at me, expressionless.

"West?"

"Leave me alone." His words were low and toneless.

"No." I stepped between his parted thighs.

"Leave me alone," he repeated, lifting the cup in his hands to his lips.

"Never."

"I don't want you here, Lena. We have nothing to say to each other."

His words sliced through me, but I'd expected them, so I was prepared.

"Too bad. I'm not leaving."

"Fucking go." He lifted the cup again, and I knocked it from his hand. I ignored the shriek of surprise from the girl sitting next to him as the cold liquid splashed on her legs. That was the least of my concerns.

"I'm not leaving until you speak to me."

He finally raised his gaze to meet mine, half-lidded and glassy, and I stumbled backwards at the look in his eyes. Oh. He was still angry. Really, really angry. Underneath the anger, though, I could see the hurt and confusion, and that killed me.

I crouched down in front of him. Tentatively, I reached out and placed a hand on his thigh. He stiffened but didn't push me away, which was something, at least.

"Need another drink," he slurred, his head falling back. "I can't deal with you right now."

"West, please."

"Just fucking leave me alone." He closed his eyes.

Right.

Rising to my feet, I took him in, leaning back on the sofa all dark and sexy, tension thrumming through his body despite the amount of alcohol he'd clearly ingested.

Then, I turned my back and walked away.

Only as far as the bar. I had to get him to listen to me somehow.

When I returned, I handed him a large plastic cup brimming with a clear liquid. "Drink this."

Surprisingly, he took it from me. Tipping it to his lips, he took a large gulp, then grimaced. "What the fuck is this?"

"Water. Drink it."

I could've sworn a growl came from his throat, as he levelled me with a dark look. But he downed the rest of the water, then threw the cup into the crowd.

Standing in front of him, I eyed him carefully. He'd stopped telling me to leave, but now he was acting like I wasn't even here. I'd never seen him like this before, and I honestly didn't know what to do.

Fuck it. Stepping forwards, I straddled him, sinking down onto his thighs.

His hard muscles tensed underneath my legs. "Get off me."

"No."

"You've done enough. I don't want you here, *Mercury*," he practically snarled.

Yep. He was seriously pissed off with me. "Too bad. I'm not leaving until I've said what I came here to say."

"Leave me the fuck alone." He lifted me off him and climbed to his feet, staggering away through the crowd. As if I was going to let him get away from me that easily. I stalked through the crush of bodies in the direction of the doors.

When I reached the outside of the building, I stopped dead when I saw him leaning against the wall. He blinked a few times, finally focusing on my face, his eyes clearer at last. Hopefully the fresh air and the water had helped. "Go on, then. Say whatever it was you wanted to say."

"Can we get a coffee first? I think we need to sober up.

By we, I mean you. You need to stop trying to chase your problems away with alcohol."

He snorted at that. "Whatever."

I stared at him, arms folded across my chest, until he gave a heavy sigh. "Fine. I'll grab one from the machine."

A few minutes later, he returned with two coffee cups in his hand, one of which he handed to me wordlessly.

A tiny ember of hope lit inside me. And when I tasted the slightly bitter, chocolatey flavour of my favourite mocha, the hope flared.

We sipped our coffees in silence, walking in the direction of the car park. "Where do you want to talk?" I ventured, stopping close to my car.

He shrugged, not answering.

"Okay, here is good, then." I hopped up onto the low stone wall that ran down the side of the car park. He stood, facing me, wariness in his deep aquamarine eyes.

Taking a deep breath, I began to relay my story, explaining why I'd reacted the way I had to him. I didn't stumble, I didn't falter—I needed to make him understand. His expression morphed from shock, to horror, to anger, to disbelief, and by the time I'd finished speaking, he was leaning against the wall next to me, breathing heavily and gripping the stone so tightly that his knuckles were white.

"Fucking hell," he said shakily. His eyes met mine, wide and distressed. "How could you have let me touch you at all?"

I shook my head, the sudden lump in my throat leaving me unable to answer.

"I'm so sorry. *So* sorry." He lifted his arm as if to touch me, but hesitated and let it fall to his side.

That small movement broke me, and the tears that I'd been able to hold at bay gathered in my eyes.

Without knowing it, he continued to twist the knife. "I think it's better that we don't see each other for a while," he said in a low mutter.

I broke a little bit more. The thing was? He was probably right. "Okay." My voice came out as a whisper. "And, West, for what it's worth, I'm so sorry I didn't tell you I was Mercury."

"No. We're not talking about this now." He shook his head emphatically, then released his death grip on the wall and began to back away from me. "Get in the car. Text Winter or Cass as soon as you get home." A heavy breath escaped him as he lifted his hand, and the moment felt final. "Bye, Lena."

He waited until I was safely inside my car.

Then he was gone, taking a piece of me with him.

17

weston

Two weeks had passed, and I hadn't spoken to Lena, but I was living back at home, and my relationship with my friends was back on track. Yeah, I still had some resentment and hurt there, but it helped to see how cut up they'd been about it all. Cade, in particular.

"Here." My brother slid a large mug of coffee across the table to me as I sat, rubbing at my brow. My headache wouldn't shift, and I wasn't making any headway with investigating this guy. "What's up?"

"Just not getting anywhere with this guy, Martin Smith. Have you heard of him? He works for Alstone Holdings, but everything about him is perfect. Too perfect. Not even a parking fine."

He lowered himself into the seat next to me. "I vaguely recognise the name but couldn't tell you anything about him. So Dad's asked you to investigate because he can't pin anything on this guy legally?"

"Yeah, pretty much. Except he doesn't know it's me investigating."

He studied me. "Don't you think you should tell him?"

"No."

"But you had a problem with the fact that Lena was keeping her identity as Mercury hidden."

"That's not the same," I snapped.

"Isn't it?" He raised a brow.

"Okay, look, I'll tell him afterwards, okay? But you know I won't be able to get anything done if he knows it's me. You, you're the responsible older one, but me? He doesn't see me as capable. *Yet*."

"That's also true." Leaning back in his chair, he kicked up his feet and rested them on the edge of the desk. "You want some help? I've got your back. You're my brother, and you know what? You are fucking capable. You're a computer genius, and we wouldn't have got anywhere with the whole Christine thing without you."

"Feet off my desk," I told him, and he stuck his tongue out at me. Shaking my head, I tutted. "And people think you're the mature one."

"Fuck off." He grinned at me. "Wanna follow this Smith guy and see where he goes? Or track him down at Dad's work?"

"I do..." I glanced at my phone to check the time. "I've got to meet James at the uni library soon, want to come? We can check out Martin Smith afterwards."

"James who?" A suspicious expression crossed his face, and I couldn't help my smirk.

"Granville."

"Fucking Granville," he muttered. "Why?" He threw his head back, staring at the ceiling as if it had the answers.

I laughed. "Because I want to talk to him about Lena. You know, say thanks and all that. Cassius thanked him already, but y'know. She's our best mate's sister. We've known her all our lives. We owe him our thanks."

His expression sobered as he lowered his head. "Oh, yeah." Lena had asked Winter to give the others the details of what had happened to her. Winter had told me that talking about it and people knowing had really helped Lena. It made me sick to think of what she'd been through, and despite the fact that we'd both fucked up things between us, I owed James my thanks. I didn't even want to think about what might have happened if he hadn't been there.

"Let's go now. I'm not getting anything done here." Standing, I stretched. "We're taking my car, by the way."

"Mine."

"Mine."

We argued all the way to the front door and ended up driving separately since, apparently, both of us were stubborn bastards.

In the library, I met James up on the top floor, dragging along my unwilling brother. Before we could even sit down, Caiden opened his big mouth. "I would say it's a pleasure, Granville, but we both know that would be a lie."

James rolled his eyes. "Seeing your face always brightens my day, Cavendish."

My brother bit back a smile, and I laughed. At this point, I was 80 percent sure that they were just pretending to dislike each other.

We threw ourselves into the seats at the small table James had commandeered, and I took charge of the conversation before they could trade any more insults. "I came here to meet you today because I wanted to say thanks for what you did for Lena."

Understanding crossed his face. "I did what anyone would have done."

"Even so, thanks."

"Yeah, thanks," Caiden added reluctantly, after I kicked him under the table.

James nodded. "No thanks necessary."

None of us mentioned the other elephant in the room. The other person who had been there for Lena. James' cousin, Tim Hyde, who had passed away in a tragic accident. But we were all sorry. Sorry about all the animosity between our families. Maybe if things had been different, if our families hadn't been pitted against one another as rivals, we might have been friends.

Maybe.

We sat in a kind of awkward silence for a couple of minutes, before Caiden sighed loudly. "Arsenal's chances aren't looking very good after Sunday's performance."

James raised a brow. "Sorry, were you watching the same match I was, Chelsea boy? Your team can't even manage one match without someone pretending to be injured."

Then, somehow, we managed to spend the next thirty minutes in a light-hearted discussion about football, and Caiden and James managed not to kill each other.

It was a miracle.

Outside the main office of Alstone Holdings, Caiden and I leaned against a wall and tried to work out a plan of action.

"Okay, the car park has cameras, so we can't do anything suspicious. I'm thinking we wait till Smith comes out, then follow him into the car park, and then I can get his plates. From there, I should be able to get his address details."

Cade nodded. "This would be so much easier if we just asked Dad, you know."

"I know, but I don't want him involved. The fact he's even hired Kryptos to begin with means he wants to keep this quiet."

"Yeah, I know." He glanced at me. "Do you even know what this guy looks like?"

"I have his company ID photo…" I thumbed through my phone to find it. "It's kind of grainy, though."

We both studied the image. A headshot of a grey-haired guy, nondescript, wearing glasses with thin wire rims.

"Hmm. We need to get a closer look. Let's go inside." Before I could reply, Caiden was strolling confidently through the doors of Alstone Holdings, and I had no choice but to follow him.

"Afternoon, Darren." He inclined his head at the secu-rity guy standing next to the front desk. "Is my dad in?"

Darren stared at him, bemused, but he nodded. "What are you doing here?"

It was a fair question. We hadn't exactly shown up here unannounced before, so I guess our sudden appearance was a surprise.

"Didn't you hear? It's bring your kids to work day," I threw in, and Darren gave me an unimpressed look.

"I must've missed that memo."

"Whatever. Are you going to let us in, or do I need to call my dad?" Caiden made a show out of pulling his phone from his pocket.

"No, no need to do that," he said hastily, swiping his card to let us up. "Cathy, will you call Mr. Cavendish and let him know his sons are here to see him?"

The receptionist nodded, and I gave her a cheeky wink, making her blush.

"Do you have to flirt with every woman you see?" Caiden muttered, shaking his head at me.

"Yep."

While Caiden headed in the direction of my dad's office, I slowed my steps, discreetly attempting to peer into various offices, but there were so many rooms and desks it was like looking for a needle in a haystack.

I stared around me, spotting the water cooler in the corner of the room. A young, pretty woman stood in front of it, filling a bottle.

Perfect.

"Hi." I stopped in front of her, giving her my most charming smile. She smiled and blushed.

"Hi." She gave me a thorough once-over, and I grinned. This would be easy. I hoped. "You don't work here."

"What gave it away?" I stepped closer. "My lack of a suit?"

"That, and the fact that you look like a model. You're far too gorgeous to be stuck working in an office."

I laughed at that. If only she knew that she was talking to one of the heirs to Alstone Holdings. This would be my workplace as soon as I graduated from Alstone College. Since she hadn't recognised me, I could only surmise that she was new.

"I could say the same about you." I widened my grin, piling on the charm as she blushed again. "Would you be able to help me with something? I'm looking for an employee. A Mr. Martin Smith, works in finance. Would you happen to know where I could find him?"

At her enthusiastic nod, I almost sighed in relief but stopped myself at the last minute. "His office is through those doors there—" She pointed to the doors at the corner of the room. "—and down the corridor. Second door on the right, I think."

"Thank you." Backing away from her now that I had the information I wanted, I blew her a kiss and turned away.

When I was out in the corridor, I was suddenly struck with the thought that I hadn't been interested in her. At all. My dick hadn't even stirred, and she'd been young and gorgeous; normally, that would be enough for me to at least get her number. I frowned. When was the last time a girl had made my dick hard? When was the last time I'd *been* with a girl?

Fuck. I slumped against the wall, scrubbing my hand over my face. The answer to the first question was Lena... and I guess that also answered my second question.

I was in big trouble.

But I couldn't think about that now. I had a shady finance guy to catch.

His office was easy enough to find, now I knew where it was. Making a snap decision, I knocked at the door. At the muffled "come in," I swung the door wide and took a good look at him. Grey, swept-back hair, those thin, wire-rimmed glasses perched on a slightly hooked nose, and harsh lines on his face making him appear severe. My senses immediately went on to high alert. Maybe it was just a gut feeling, but there was something off about this guy.

"Sorry, wrong room." I closed the door as quickly as I could and headed off to find my brother and my dad.

"By reducing the packaging, we can not only save money, but transport roughly 30 percent more goods, meaning more profit," my dad was saying as I entered his room without knocking. Caiden's head was bent over my dad's computer, both of them intent on the screen, as my dad tapped on a chart with a silver pen.

"Makes sense. Did you look at the stuff I emailed you?"

My dad smiled proudly. "The eco transport company? I did, and I have a meeting set up with the director next month."

Listening to their conversation, a combination of bitterness and sadness filled me. My dad was so proud of Caiden. I knew he saw him as a leader. And I didn't begrudge him that, at all—my brother was a born leader. Me, though? I knew my dad still saw me as the happy-go-lucky kid who needed protecting. Maybe it was the curse of being the younger sibling, but I'd never felt more redundant than I did right then. I wanted my dad to be proud of me. Maybe, if I could crack this thing with Martin Smith, I could prove myself to him.

My dad looked up, noticing me, and a wide, genuine smile spread across his face. "Both my sons? This is a pleasant surprise."

I returned his smile, the bitterness dissipating as I took in his face. We fell into an easy conversation about university, and by the time the workday had ended, I was much more positive. My dad was working late, no surprise there, so Caiden and I said our goodbyes and stepped outside. Perfect fucking timing, since Martin Smith was exiting the building right then.

"That's him," I murmured to my brother, and he gave a sharp nod before we trailed him at a distance, all the way into the car park where I pulled out my phone and set the camera to snap a few discreet photos as we walked past. He got into a silver Mercedes saloon car, slinging his briefcase into the seat next to him before starting up the engine.

"Do you have the number plate?"

"Yep."

"Let's bring this guy down."

18

lena

"These tips are ridiculous. We're not getting anywhere." I blew out a frustrated breath as James kicked at the ground next to me.

"I know," he muttered, his gaze constantly shifting around us as we stood in the grimy alley behind a warehouse that lay to the east of Alstone. I knew he was uncomfortable, and to be honest, I'd rather he wasn't involved, but he'd ended up being tangled up in all this when he'd stumbled on his uncle, Roland Hyde, placing bets on one of the fights. The same uncle that was currently waiting on his trial for fraud and embezzlement, among other things.

The fights in question? Dog fights. Underneath Alstone's pristine surface was a seedy underbelly, and illegal dog fighting was something that I'd never, ever be okay with. I'd made it my mission to uncover the organisers of this and bring them down, and I wouldn't allow myself to fail. James had been with me on a few of my recon missions—there as my backup-slash-getaway driver, although I preferred to work alone. It was easier to remain undetected when there was only one of you.

I think James still felt a sense of responsibility towards me in a way, though. We hadn't really interacted much since he'd come to my rescue, not until I'd started investigating the dog fighting. I'd always be grateful to him, but I think we both wanted to put that situation behind us. But after he'd found out that his uncle was interested in the fights, we had a common cause, and over the past year we'd become…not friends, exactly, but friendly, I guess you could say.

I appreciated his backup, but last Halloween, we'd received a tip-off that a dog fight was taking place on an industrial ground over in Highnam, and let's just say, I had first-hand experience of being inside a huge rubbish bin, when James had accidentally made our presence known by managing to fall over a bike. I mean, who the fuck trips over a bike? It wasn't even lying down—it had been standing up, chained to a lamppost. Anyway, needless to say, we'd missed that opportunity and hadn't managed to come close again since.

"That's all of it."

We both stiffened at the voice coming from the end of the alley, and I ducked down, hopefully undetected with the large recycling bins that blocked us from view. I angled my phone around the edge of the bin, my camera already recording, just in case we managed to pick up anything useful. Watching the view through my phone screen, I made out two figures silhouetted against the streetlamp. One handed something to the other. Cash, possibly? It was hard to tell from a distance.

"I trust you. You know what'll happen, though, if you've short-changed me."

"It's all there," the first voice insisted. "Martin—uh, Mr. Smith, counted it personally."

"Good. In that case, you can expect the delivery on Thursday. I think you'll be pleased. This batch is from Romania. Same family as the last. Highly trained, vicious little bastards."

My heart sped up at the words. They had to be talking about the dogs. *Had* to be. So far, these people had been like ghosts—moving from location to location, leaving no traces behind. I knew some of the Alstone elite actually enjoyed the dog fights, much to my disgust. The fights were normally filmed, and bets were placed on the dogs—I'd seen it with my own eyes. No one seemed to be bothered about stopping it, so I had to take a stand.

The voices grew fainter, and a moment later, I heard the sound of an engine starting up.

Once the guys were gone and I was back in my car, having parted ways with James, I googled the name of the guy they'd mentioned. After narrowing down my search to the local area, I had it.

He worked at Alstone Holdings.

A slow smile spread across my face. Weston had been giving me the silent treatment, but now I had an excuse to contact him. He may have written us off, but I wasn't going to give him up without a fight. Not now I'd had a taste of him. I *knew* we could get past the mess we'd made of things.

I just had to convince him to try.

Opening up my Kryptos app, I sent a code yellow alert to Weston. I shouldn't abuse our alert system, but I was fairly sure he wouldn't talk to me otherwise. In under five minutes, I got a response.

Nitro: ???
Me: Hi, I'm Mercury.

There was a long pause, during which I held my breath, and finally, a reply appeared on my screen.

Nitro: Hi. I'm Nitro.

My heart leapt, and a smile spread across my face. He was playing along. Maybe there was still hope for us. I was done with keeping my distance, done with being scared. I'd dealt with what had happened with him, and if it happened again, I'd deal with it again. I was strong. I'd made it through the fire and survived the burns.

And the way he'd kissed me...there *had* to be hope.

Me: Nice to meet you. Virtually

This time, the pause stretched out, so I quickly added another message.

Me: WYR meet someone who had something important to show you, or stay at home?
Nitro: WYR be betrayed by your family or your friends?
Me: WYR forgive people or continue to act like a stubborn bastard?
Nitro: Too soon to joke about that

I sighed. We weren't getting anywhere with this conversation.

Me: I have something important to show you. Can you meet me?

Another long pause. Tapping out a rhythm with my

fingers on my steering wheel, I forced myself not to push. Finally, my patience was rewarded with another message.

Nitro: Where?
Me: Anywhere you want.
Nitro: Castle.
Me: I'll be there in 10.

He signed out of the chat, and I started up my car.

19

lena

Pulling up at the Alstone Castle ruins, I saw that Weston's car was already parked. Nervous excitement thrummed through me, and I relished the feeling. As I headed over to the ruined castle, picking my way between the boulders that lay scattered in the grass, he appeared on the clifftop. Standing there in dark sweatpants and a royal blue hoodie, his hair ruffled by the breeze, he looked so gorgeous that my breath caught in my throat and my heart beat faster. But it wasn't just the way he looked. I loved his upbeat personality, his kindness and generosity, his charm, and his smile...fuck, that smile was lethal.

In short, for me, he was all I'd ever wanted.

He was everything.

"Hi," I said when I reached him, and when his gorgeous mouth curved into that smile I loved, I couldn't help myself. Closing the final bit of distance between us, I stood as close as I dared, not quite touching him, but I could feel the heat from his body against mine.

Deep blue pools swirled through with green and grey met my gaze. There was no longer any anger in them.

Maybe...was there a tentative hope?

My breath stuttered, and my heart pounded out of my throat.

Taking what felt like the biggest risk of my life, I reached up and hesitantly pressed a soft kiss to his lips.

He froze, and I pulled back, my cheeks flaming. What the fuck had I been thinking? We hadn't even spoken for two weeks, and how did—

My racing thoughts were interrupted by his hand reaching around the back of my neck, holding me still, and then his lips were on mine again.

The slide of his mouth against mine and his hand gripping me, holding me in place with such strength but so carefully...it was like a puzzle piece clicked into place deep inside me, and I knew with complete certainty that this man would never do anything to physically hurt me.

A shiver ran through my body, and he pulled me closer, trailing kisses across my jaw and down my neck. "Is this okay for you?" he murmured against my skin, his voice a husky rasp, and the fact that he was taking so much care brought a lump to my throat.

"More than okay," I assured him, pressing closer, and in reply, he brought his other hand up to span my waist while he lightly scraped his teeth along my earlobe. A soft moan escaped my throat, and he nipped me harder, his grip on me tightening.

Bolts of sensation peppered my skin, like nothing I'd ever felt before. There was a kind of euphoric high that I got when I outsmarted an opponent in martial arts training, or when I managed to crack a high-level security or software code. But this...this was pure, addictive pleasure. A high that I never wanted to come down from.

All too soon, though, it ended. Weston drew back from

me, releasing his grip. Staring at me through heavy-lidded eyes, he licked his lips. We were both silent for a moment, unsure how to navigate this situation between us.

Running a hand through his hair, he blew out a heavy breath. "We need to talk."

Emboldened by his kiss, the words tumbled from my mouth before I could think them through. "Can't we kiss some more?"

My hopeful suggestion was met with a firm head shake. "Nope. You need to tell me what was so important that you sent me a code yellow alert. Then, *maybe*, we'll kiss after." A smirk tugged at the corners of his mouth, and I rolled my eyes.

"Fine. I guess."

He headed over to a large flat rock that was situated in the courtyard area of the castle, with a makeshift firepit in front of it. He dropped onto the rock, stretching out his legs in front of him, so I went and straddled him, threading my arms around his neck. Fuck it. If he didn't want me near him, he could tell me.

"Lena..." His tone was filled with warning, and I gave him an innocent smile.

"Let's talk."

He sighed heavily, but his arms came around my waist, and I bit my lip to hide my smile.

"Okay," I started. "Does the name Martin Smith mean anything to you?"

"What?" His whole body stiffened beneath me.

Jackpot.

"You know him?"

"What does he mean to you?" Weston countered.

Leaning forwards, I placed a kiss to the side of his mouth before leaning back. I'd always held myself back, but

121

now? Now this missing piece had clicked into place, I wanted him, and I didn't want there to be any doubt about my intentions. His lips curved up again, and I drank in the sight before I turned serious.

"Do you remember that I was looking into dog fighting?"

He nodded.

"Okay, well...just watch the video." Pulling my phone out, I held it between us, angling the screen towards him.

We both watched in silence until the video was finished, and then his eyes met mine, his gaze troubled. "I've been investigating Martin Smith for my dad, although my dad only knows he's hired Kryptos, not that I'm involved. This Smith guy works at Alstone Holdings, and while I don't have anything on him yet, I will." He finished speaking with a confident tone, and I didn't doubt his words.

"It seems like we're after the same guy. Want to work together to bring him down?"

It felt like I held my breath forever, waiting for his reply. But when it came, it was worth the wait.

"Yeah."

"Thank you." My words were breathed into the air between us, and he inclined his head forwards, just enough that it rested against mine.

Wanting to explain further, I began, "I've been investigating the dog fighting with James—"

"No," he growled, his tone hard and possessive.

"Sorry, what?" I'd never heard him speak like that before, and I wasn't sure what to make of it.

"Fuck. Is this how Cade felt?" he muttered to himself, before directing his gaze at mine. "I don't...whatever this thing is between us, we need to allow it time to...uh, develop." His adamant tone was gone, replaced by uncertainty, and honestly? It made me melt. "I don't want you hanging out with other guys. Alone." His eyes narrowed, daring me to disagree, and my stomach flipped. "I...it's not safe."

"Okay," I agreed easily, and he relaxed against me.

"Okay. Good."

We stared at each other for a moment before I dropped my head to his shoulder. "This is so awkward," I mumbled into his neck, feeling him laugh against me.

"Yeah. Let's just take it one day at a time, okay?" His confidence had returned, and he stroked his hand up my back, making me shiver under his touch.

"That sounds good to me." Suddenly shy, I directed my words at his jaw, unable to meet his gaze.

"Lena." The seriousness of his tone had my eyes snapping to his. "I don't know what I'm doing here."

"That makes two of us."

His hand came up to stroke my hair back from my face, and he cupped my chin. "Yeah. But I mean, I don't want to hurt you, okay? You need to tell me if I do anything you're uncomfortable with."

Oh, fuck. Stupid tears filled my eyes.

"I don't want to be broken anymore," I choked out. "*Please*, West." I couldn't even articulate my feelings in my own head, let alone speak them out loud.

His eyes widened, filled with so much compassion that I couldn't bear it.

"Fuck," he breathed. "Is that really how you see yourself?" His arms tightened around me, and he pulled me into him. I let my head rest against his shoulder as he continued speaking. "You know what I see when I look at you? I see someone who's been through unimaginable shit, come through the other side, and given it a giant fuck-you. You're

123

strong, Lena. So strong. Not only that, you're a bloody genius. The shit you do as Mercury? Honestly, it leaves me in awe." Gripping my chin again, he gently tilted my head up so I had no choice but to meet his eyes. "And on top of all that?" His gaze went soft, so soft that I melted against him as his voice dropped to a whisper. "You're beautiful. Inside and out. So wild and untamed, so fucking far out of my league that I'm just waiting for you to come to your senses."

My. Jaw. Dropped.

What was I supposed to say to that?

20

weston

Her mouth opened and closed, and I barely stifled my grin. I'd made Lena Drummond speechless. I meant what I'd said, though. And I had to tread carefully. Not only had she been through shit that had clearly had a major effect on her, but she was my best mate's sister, and I doubted he'd be very understanding if I fucked around with her. Not that I wanted to fuck around with her. No, I needed to get things straight in my head.

I knew two things, right at that moment, holding her against me. One, I didn't care anymore about the fact that she'd hidden her identity as Mercury from me. And two? Yeah, I could admit it now—I was really attracted to her. My dick was in total agreement with my head, and it took all of my control to stay calm, to not treat her like one of my conquests. Lena was fucking special, and I wasn't about to mess up any potential...whatever...between us.

With that in mind, I lifted her off me, setting her down next to me on the rock. She gave me a bit of a confused look but didn't say anything.

"Tell me everything you know about the dog fighting."

Her face cleared, and she began to speak.

As she recounted the details that had led us to this point, I began to build up a picture in my head. I wasn't stupid—I'd heard the rumours of dog fighting being used as entertainment, and I knew that when Christine had been alive, she'd allowed the live fights to be streamed at her parties. Not out in the open of course, but there were always the discreet rooms away from the main party, packed with those of the Alstone elite who wanted a more sordid kind of entertainment. It wasn't right, but I guess I'd buried my head in the sand about it, especially since at the time, both my brother and I had wanted as little as possible to do with my dad and his relationship with Christine.

Lena had been attempting to track down the local organisers of these fights, as and when she had a chance, in between school and home life and whatever other shit she had going on. Her intel had led her to what was supposed to be an exchange of actual animals but had turned out to be an exchange of money, and now she had this name. The name of the man I was investigating for potential financial discrepancies. With my dad's suspicions, the red flags that had been raised the minute I'd seen Martin Smith in person, and now this? I didn't have any proof, but my instincts were telling me that there was a link here.

With that in mind, I ran my hands through her hair and placed a soft kiss on Lena's mouth. My head was telling me that getting involved with her while all this shit was going on, not to mention everything she'd been through, was a bad idea. But I guess I was a selfish bastard.

"I think we should get the others involved. The boys and Winter. It's not safe for you to be going off on your own, and if there's anything that the situation with Christine taught me, it's that we're stronger together than apart."

At her hesitant nod, I smiled, and then my face fell. "Fuck. Cass."

She sighed against me. "I know. We spoke after Winter had left to find you, the night you'd gone to the hotel, and he was...I'd never seen him so cut up. Let's just say that the overprotective older-brother routine is about to get a whole lot worse, especially now he's going to find out the details of what I've been investigating."

"Yeah, that, but I also meant you and me." I forced the words from my mouth, hating them even as I said them, which just proved to me how into this girl I really was. "I think it's better if we put this on the back burner for now, until he's had time to deal with everything else."

"No." Her gorgeous mouth set in a stubborn pout. "Not happening."

"Fuck, you're stubborn." Shaking my head at her, I couldn't help the wry grin that stretched over my lips.

"Get used to it." Gone was the soft, vulnerable side that she'd shown me earlier, and in its place was the strong, fearless woman that I knew and liked. A lot. And I liked her even more now that she'd shown me her vulnerable side, shared a part of herself that she never showed to the world. Only her closest friends and family knew about it. The fact that she'd allowed Winter and Cassius to tell Caiden and Zayde what had happened to her, and the fact she'd told me herself, proved how much she saw us as worthy of her trust. She'd been slowly working her way into our group, and I just hoped she was here to stay.

Wait. What? Here to stay? Pushing down that thought,

because there was no way I was thinking of the future right now, I reminded myself that I needed to take things one day at a time.

"Okay," I said, because apparently she had me wrapped around her finger already. Was I ready to give her up, now I'd admitted that I liked her, now I'd had a taste?

The answer to that was a solid *fuck, no.* "We'll take it slow, and nothing in front of the others yet, alright?" There was going to be enough pressure as it was without having whatever was starting to happen between us be under a microscope. And as much as I loved my best mate, I knew he wouldn't be able to help himself interfering.

"Deal." Then she fucking shook my hand, making me laugh. After a second's hesitation, she laughed, too.

"That was lame, wasn't it?"

"Yeah, a bit."

She jabbed me in the ribs, and instead of retaliating, I pulled her into my lap, gripped the back of her neck, and slanted my mouth over hers.

Much, much later, I lifted her off me and stood, adjusting my dick, a move Lena didn't miss.

"Need some help with that?" Her tone was sultry, but I could see the flash of uncertainty in her eyes.

"Nah, I'm good. Just the effect you have on me." Giving her a cheeky wink, which resulted in an almost shy smile from her, I attempted to think of anything to deflate my hard-on. Taking it slow was going to be torture, when I was used to the opposite. But Lena wasn't just a quick fuck. So... "Wanna get it over with? Tell the others about the dog fighting now? Then go through the evidence we both have and see if we can find anything that matches up?"

"I guess so."

"No need to sound so happy about it. Come on, follow me back?"

"Alright."

21

lena

Although it was a detour, we drove back to my house first so I could grab an overnight bag and my laptop. Leaving my car behind, I slid into the passenger seat of Weston's DBS, letting the scent of leather and new car surround me. As Weston drove, I couldn't help noticing the way he kept sneaking sidewards glances at me. Every time he did it, my heart skipped a beat. This still didn't seem real, that he was actually into me. How was it possible?

When we arrived back at the house that he shared with the rest of the Four and Winter, there were no cars outside.

"I thought everyone would be home," Weston commented as he unlocked the front door. Stepping back to direct me inside, he continued talking. "This is good, actually. We can go through our evidence before they get back. Wanna drop your bag upstairs and meet me in the computer room?"

After dumping my bag in the guest room, I changed into a baggy black hoodie that almost came to my knees, fleece-lined and more like a blanket than a hoodie. Leaving my legs bare other than my fluffy socks, I padded back downstairs to Weston.

He was already at work, inputting lines of code that were scrolling across the screen and navigating to our secure server. When I entered the room, he didn't even look up, too intent on what he was doing.

Yep, I knew that feeling. When I was engrossed in my work, the outside world stopped existing for me. Instead of disturbing him, I locked the door behind me, then pulled up a chair and set up my laptop on his desk, plugging it in to one of the giant monitors so that we'd have a better view.

"Here." He finally spoke after we'd been pulling information in silence for around twenty minutes. "Come and look at this."

Sliding out of my chair, I went and stood next to his, peering closely at the screen.

"See…here." Without warning, he tugged me down onto his lap and banded his arm around me.

I was suddenly so aware of him. His body at my back, the way he held me firmly in place, his warm breath hitting my ear as he leaned his head over my shoulder to speak. As he moved his other hand, clicking the mouse and highlighting the phone records of Martin Smith on the screen, it took everything I had to concentrate on what he was telling me.

"What am I looking at?" Oh, bloody hell. The rasp in my voice betrayed me, and I shifted in his lap. Since our bodies were pressed together so closely, I didn't miss his sharp intake of breath or the growing hardness I felt beneath me.

"This text thread here," he said in a rough, low tone, moving his hand from around my waist and down onto my thigh, on top of the thick fabric of my hoodie. He left it there, unmoving, until I relaxed back against him. "See? This message is most likely coded, but it could refer to the dog purchases."

As he spoke, he began to run his fingers up and down my thigh in light, teasing touches.

I. Was. On. Fire.

My thighs clenched. As his fingertips closed around the bottom of my hoodie, I moved my legs wider in a silent invitation, the ache between my legs undeniable. I'd been in love with this boy for so long, but the desperate craving for his touch... This? This was new.

His lips touched my ear as he spoke softly. "This message is dated from the week before you saw the two guys meet." He dragged the fabric of my hoodie slowly up, all the way to the top of my thighs. My heart was racing, my breath stuttering as he unclasped his fingers from the fabric and laid them on my bare leg. "I don't know who the recipient is, but read the message."

How? What? My brain was overloaded, all my senses directed towards the sensation of his hand trailing up my thigh.

"The message?" He laughed softly, amused at my lack of attention.

"How...can...you...expect me to concentrate?" My head fell back against his shoulder.

"I fucking love how responsive you are." His teeth nipped at my earlobe. Then, "If there's anything you feel uncomfortable with, tell me, and I'll stop straight away."

Warmth flowed through me at his words, because I knew he meant them. I trusted him, and for that reason, my reply easily fell from my lips.

"Don't stop."

"I won't, *if* you concentrate. What do you notice about this message?"

Dammit! Why was he torturing me this way?

His fingers paused, touching the band of my underwear with the barest pressure. An involuntary whimper tore from my throat. "Stop fucking teasing me," I whispered.

"Read the message, Lena."

With an effort, I focused my attention on the screen. The words swam together, and I blinked, then blinked again, gathering the shreds of my self-control so I could focus.

Martin: 3 parcels, prepaid. Post them at the usual place. Thom is expecting them.

"Um." I licked my lips. "Parcels must refer to the dogs?"

"Good." His voice dropped, and he dragged one finger over my clit, down my slit, and back up again.

"Oh, fuck." My hips involuntarily arched forwards. How the fuck was I meant to survive Weston Cavendish? He was incinerating me and he'd barely even touched me. I had no idea it could be like this. No idea *he'd* be like this.

"So..." he continued, his finger slipping under the fabric, making direct contact with my skin. "Do you think this refers to the meeting you intercepted?"

"Yes," I moaned, moving my legs wider, not even recognising myself in this moment.

"This message, too." Leaning forwards, he reached out and clicked the mouse, scrolling through the records to a highlighted conversation. At the same time he opened it, he pushed his index finger into me.

My whole body stiffened, warring with my mind.

"Breathe, baby. It's me." He pressed the softest kiss to

the side of my throat and curled his finger inside me. His breathing grew heavier, the huskiness in his voice proving that I was affecting him. "You see how they mention parcels again? This one has a date."

"Y-yes," I managed to say, as his hand moved, stroking over my clit, while his finger moved in and out of me, sliding through my wetness.

"This number's the same as the other one. I've run it through the system, but no hits. Probably a burner phone." Another finger joined the first, making me gasp. His voice continued to rasp in my ear as he kept up his movements, increasing the pace bit by bit. "What do you think? Should we intercept the next meeting?"

"Y-*Ahhhhh, fuck*." My pussy clamped around his finger as the orgasm hit me out of nowhere, blinding in its intensity.

The first orgasm I'd had that hadn't been self-induced.

As I came back down, I was aware of the tiniest things. A small fly, perched on the corner of the computer monitor in front of me. The faint scent of lemon, slightly antiseptic, presumably from whatever cleaning products had been used in here. The soft slide of fabric as Weston withdrew from me and adjusted my clothes. Weston's chest, rapidly rising and falling against my back.

Weston's hard, hard cock, pressed against my ass.

All I wanted to do right then was to make him feel as good as he'd made me feel.

On shaky legs, I stood and turned to face him, letting myself collapse back against the desk. My gaze took him in, the way he watched me intently, his pupils more dilated than I'd ever seen before, and...fuck it. I bypassed the rest of him to zero in on the result of our...proximity. His hardness, straining against the material of his sweatpants.

My mouth watered. Sucking dick had never been high on my agenda. But now, it was right at the fucking top.

"Put your fingers in your mouth."

He swallowed hard, his lids lowering to half-mast. "These ones?"

As he lifted the fingers that had just been inside of me, I nodded.

"Yes."

Without taking his eyes from me, he slid them into his mouth.

"I need to suck your cock." I could barely get the words out.

Hesitation entered his eyes. "Are you—"

"Don't ask me if I'm sure."

He must've recognised the steel in my tone, because he nodded once, then gripped his waistband, and lifting himself slightly, tugged down his sweatpants.

Oh. Fuck.

Nothing, and I mean nothing, could have prepared me for the sight of Weston's cock. I hadn't had personal experience, but I'd watched porn, and his long, thick hardness was mouth-watering, hotter than anything I'd ever seen.

Before I could allow myself to be intimidated, or worse, talk myself out of it, I sank to my knees and gripped the base. He hissed through his teeth, his cock jerking in my grip, but his hands remained at his sides, holding on to the sides of his chair tightly as he allowed me to take things at my own pace.

Leaning forwards, I kissed the top, my tongue automatically swiping across my lips, tasting his precum. I hummed in approval, then, still holding the base, licked around the tip with a long drag of my tongue.

"Lena." His voice was guttural, and right then, I felt

more powerful than I ever had before. To know that I was on my knees, yet he was the one falling apart...it was insane and addictive, and I wanted more.

"How do you like it?" I stared up at him from beneath my lashes. "Like this?" Channelling what I knew from porn and hoping it wasn't all a lie, I lowered my head to encompass his thickness, sliding my free hand along his inner thighs and carefully cupping his balls.

"Fucking hell," he mumbled, and I smiled. My jaw already ached, he was so fucking thick, but I craved his responses. Just to test things out, I flicked my tongue across the underside of the head as I sucked him down again, and I was rewarded with a heavy groan and his hands white-knuckling the sides of his chair as he fought to remain still while I worked him over. The textures, the sensations, and the flavour of him overwhelmed me, and I wanted more. More of him.

"Lena." His hands were in my hair, tugging my head upwards, and almost as soon as I released him, his hand went to his cock, right above where mine still gripped him, and he came, hard and fast, his cum painting my hoodie and the floor.

When he'd recovered, he looked at the mess he'd made and winced. "Sorry."

"I'm not." Rocking back on my heels, I smiled up at him, satisfied. "By the way? If the computer thing doesn't work out, you could consider a career in porn."

He stared at me for a moment, and then a huge grin spread across his face, his eyes sparkling. "I'll take that as a compliment."

"You should. You could take someone's eye out with that thing."

"It's my weapon of mass destruction."

Suddenly we were both laughing, and he was pulling me up and into his lap. "You're a bad girl, Lena Drummond."

"Me?" I raised a brow.

His lips skimmed over mine. "Fuck, yeah. And I love it."

22

weston

My back rested against a huge beanbag, my laptop balanced on my outstretched legs as I pulled up the relevant screen. Rather than crowding into the computer room, or the spy room, as Winter called it, we'd assembled in the lounge, and my laptop was currently connected to the huge TV that hung on the wall. We hadn't been able to collect a huge amount of data yet, but the fact that Martin Smith was connected to the dog fighting was exactly the breakthrough I needed. The fact was, all I'd had to go on up until now was my dad's gut instinct, but maybe now we could pin something on him.

And it was all thanks to Lena. I glanced over at the sofa where she was curled up next to Winter with a mug of tea clasped in her hands. Her eyes met mine, and she quickly averted her gaze, staring into the cup of tea as if it was the most fascinating thing ever. Her cheeks flushed, and I bit back a smile at the effect I was having on her. Maybe I was completely dumb, but she said she'd been into me for years, and I'd had no idea. Not until recently.

Earlier had been...unplanned, but so fucking good. I had no clue what I was doing, but I was getting good at reading her, so I went with what I thought was right. Making her concentrate on the screen while I touched her—I wanted to stop her getting lost in her head, and she hadn't had a chance to think about anything else other than that and the pleasure I was bringing her. Afterwards, when she'd sucked my cock, she'd completely taken me by surprise. I was willing to bet, based on the things she'd told me and implied, that she hadn't sucked dick before, but fuuuuck. Her gorgeous eyes staring up at me, her movements that lacked finesse but were full of her usual confidence and so fucking good...yeah, we'd be doing that again. And again.

Fuck. I shuffled on the floor, glad that my laptop was hiding my growing boner.

"You alright, mate?"

I jumped at the sound of Cassius' voice, and I knew that my cheeks were flaming red.

Yeah, mate, I'm fine. Just thinking about how your sister gives amazing head.

Divert! I said the first thing that came into my head. "What are we naming this? Operation BMSD?"

"Sounds like BDSM."

"It's Bring Martin Smith Down."

He shook his head. "Nah. That's shit, mate. What about Operation Canine? Since we're trying to rescue dogs."

"Sorry, are you five? What the fuck kind of name is that?" Caiden interrupted, and Cassius stuck his tongue out at him.

"Seriously? Why does it always end up with an argument about code names?" Winter muttered, but she couldn't hide her amusement. Instead of carrying on what I knew would be a long conversation with no resolution, I changed the subject, turning back to Cassius.

"Does the name Martin Smith mean anything to you?"

His brow creased. "I've heard the name mentioned. He works at Alstone Holdings, right?"

"That's right." I pulled up the dossier I'd put together. Technically, all I was supposed to be doing in my role as Nitro was sift through his data and see if I could find anything incriminating, but that wasn't enough for me. This was personal, involving my family and friends and the business we'd one day inherit.

I went through his information while everyone focused on the TV screen.

"Martin Smith. Age fifty-two. Divorced, no contact with his ex-wife that I can see, no kids. Lives alone. From what I can tell from his phone records, he doesn't have any close friends, although it sounds like he meets up with the same few people weekly, either at Alstone Members Club or one of the local pubs. Nothing unusual, nothing that would throw up any flags."

Lena slipped off the sofa and came to sit next to me on the floor, tugging my laptop off me. "Do you mind?"

I shook my head, letting her do whatever she wanted, my attention drawn to her face. Or more specifically, her mouth. Tamping down the urge to lean forwards and just kiss her, I attempted to focus on what she was doing.

Everything was quiet for a few minutes as she tapped on the keys, scrolling through information so fast that my eyes couldn't keep up. When she'd located our secure storage, she opened a folder, clicking through the files quickly. Eventually she cleared her throat, bringing up a video on the screen and hitting Play.

I hadn't seen this one. But I recognised the location straight away.

"Dad's house," Caiden said in a low tone, and Lena nodded. He grimaced. "When was this?"

When Lena didn't answer and the video kept playing, he fell silent. We watched as the camera panned down the corridor in my dad's home, slightly shaky. A door cracked open, and I already knew what I'd see.

The room that no one talked about.

Sure enough, a TV screen came into view, then another. One displayed a betting scoreboard, and the other showed a currently empty shallow pit, surrounded by metal bars all around. There were two hinged openings either side of the ring, which I knew the dogs would come through.

After a moment, the camera turned away from the TV screens and panned around the room, focusing on the people who were watching the TVs. It was mostly the backs of heads, but I could recognise most of them. One guy came into profile, close to the camera, and the picture went black.

Zayde hissed through his teeth, but that was the only reaction he gave at seeing his dad on-screen. Voices, too muffled to make out, sounded, and the next moment, the video ended.

"Wait, can you go back? Slow it down," I instructed.

At the same time, Winter glanced over at Lena. "What were the voices saying?"

Lena grinned. "Zayde's dad caught me loitering. I played the clueless girl, said I was looking for my brother. He seemed to buy it."

"Good thinking." Winter returned her smile as she went through the footage again, this time going frame by frame.

"There!" I held up my hand, and she paused. "Zoom in on the top left corner."

"That's him, isn't it?" Caiden spoke up, and I nodded.

Martin Smith was leaning against the wall, but his eyes weren't focused on the TV screens. He was staring intently at someone else in the room, and as Lena zoomed back out, I followed the direction of his gaze.

"Christine. I should've known," Caiden spat in disgust.

"Well, we're not getting any answers from her. She's fish food now."

"Nice thought." Caiden looked at Z and smirked, then caught Winter's expression. "Snowflake, I'm sorry. That was out of line."

She shook her head. "I know she was evil, but she was still my mother, you know?"

"I know." He tugged her onto his lap and buried his face in her hair, whispering something in her ear that caused a soft smile to appear on her face, her tension melting away.

"When was this?" Cassius asked, clearly eager to change the subject.

"This was the party where I first met Winter. Remember?" Instead of looking at him, or me, her eyes met Zayde's.

A spike of pure jealousy ripped through me at that moment, taking me aback. I remembered that night all too fucking well. Lena had shown up at the party, looking all hot and moody—her default expression until lately. It wasn't the first time I'd noticed how good she looked, but I was good at ignoring the part of me that was attracted to her, since she was Cassius' little sister, and she didn't seem to be interested in me anyway.

I'd lost track of her and had ended up playing darts with Z when Lena had appeared in the room, her hair all messed up and her makeup smeared around her face. Seeing her there had made something inside me twist uncomfortably.

When she said she needed a lift home, I'd found myself offering as soon as she'd said she couldn't get an Uber, and then Zayde had jumped in and offered his services. We'd argued a bit, and then Lena had stepped in and told me that she was choosing Z. The irrational anger and hurt I'd felt at the time rose up in me now as I watched her hold his gaze, both of their expressions unreadable.

Fuck this. I needed to get out of here.

"Getting a drink," I muttered, climbing to my feet and stalking out of the room before anyone else could comment. Once in the kitchen, I bypassed the fridge, heading outside instead. I stepped off the deck and onto the cool grass, walking across the back garden until the house was distant behind me. We'd recently had a small football pitch installed—nothing much, just a rectangle of Astroturf with a goal at either end and white lines painted on the ground. Tall lights at the sides illuminated the pitch so we could play outside during the winter when it got dark early.

There was a football lying against one of the goal nets, and I grabbed it, then began kicking it around. I stopped after a couple of minutes, because football for one didn't work. Sinking down onto the Astroturf, I rested my back against the goal, rolling the ball idly up and down my legs.

"Want to play some one-on-one?"

I looked up to see Cassius standing over me.

"Yeah, okay."

We played in silence for a while, and then Cassius spoke again. "Is everything alright?"

Guess I hadn't done a good job of hiding things. "Yeah... no. I dunno, mate. Everything's still all fucked in my head, y'know?" I sighed. "I'll be okay."

He nodded. "I know. It's a lot to deal with. I'm worried about Lena, too. After everything she's been through, I don't want her hurt anymore." Swiping the ball from the ground, he began twirling it on his finger, his gaze troubled. "I don't want her getting into trouble, either. You know how reckless she can be. We need to keep an eye on her."

"Yeah."

There was silence for a moment while he studied me with an odd expression on his face. "There's nothing going on between you and her, is there?"

I licked my lips. "Uh..."

"She doesn't need any more complications in her life right now."

For the first time, I looked my best friend dead in the eye and lied to his face.

"There's nothing going on between us."

23

lena

S omething had happened with Weston. He'd withdrawn from me, and I didn't know why. He'd said he wanted to take things slowly, but ever since we'd all gathered to discuss Martin Smith, it felt like he was avoiding me. He'd make excuses anytime we were in a situation we'd potentially be alone together, and when we were around everyone else, he treated me...not with indifference, exactly, but as he treated Kinslee—friendly, but keeping himself at a distance.

It was driving me insane.

All this had led to me making a snap decision one afternoon. I worked better alone, and that was how it was going to be if Weston wanted to keep his distance from me. It took me a couple of days to put my plan into place, and then I was ready.

First things first, I headed to my friend Raine's house. In her bedroom, I placed my phone and keys on her bedside table, next to a framed photo of her and her boyfriend, Carter, then reclined back on her bed. She grinned at me, her eyes sparkling as she held up a pair of tight black leggings.

"Ta da!" Stepping closer, she passed them to me. "So you see here, you've got these two pockets, plus the inbuilt belt. I don't know why you wanted me to line it with this wire mesh stuff, but here it is. It's removable."

I smiled at her enthusiasm. Raine designed clothes on and off, and when I'd come to her with my idea, she'd thrown herself into it head first.

"These look perfect." I stroked my fingers across the soft leather.

A shy smile spread across her face. "Thanks."

"Honestly, Raine, this is so good." I examined the tightly knit wire mesh that lined the interior of the inbuilt belt. It would block any electromagnetic signals, allowing my phone to remain undetected, if I needed it to. And more importantly, it would hide the tiny device I was planning on bringing with me that may just be the answer to our problems. If we were lucky.

"It was fun to make something different for a change. You don't even want to know how many dresses I've designed lately." She pulled a face, but I knew that she loved everything she designed.

"I'll be coming back to you for more if this works out," I told her with a grin.

We chatted for a while longer, before she had to leave to meet her boyfriend.

Then it was time for me to get to work.

Back at home, I changed into my new leggings, adding the few supplies that I needed to bring with me. Less was more when it came to this kind of thing. After strapping on my boots, I headed down to the garage and put the back seats down in my car, then loaded my bike.

I had the address memorised, so I didn't need to use the satnav to work out where I was going. When I drew close to the destination, I parked my car on the road on the darkest part of the street, outside a large, gothic-looking house. Retrieving my bike from the boot, I took a moment to think through the directions I'd memorised, then set off.

The house I was aiming for was one of a row of four-storey Georgian terraces, each one split into separate apartments. My destination was the very top floor, but I hit the buzzer for the second floor and hoped for the best.

"Yeah?" A slow, lazy drawl came from the speaker.

I hit the button to reply. "Pizza delivery for 3b."

A huff came out of the speaker. "Wrong buzzer, dude." But I heard the welcome sound of the door unlocking, and I hurried inside, quietly closing the door behind me. As I'd hoped, there was a cleaning supply cupboard under the stairs, and after easily picking the lock, I settled inside to wait.

By the time I exited the supply cupboard, stretching, the entire building was dark and silent, other than the emergency lighting that dimly illuminated the hallway. Avoiding the security cameras, which basically only focused on the external doors, I crept up the stairs, all the way to the top.

Pausing outside the door, I took a moment to regain my breath while I studied the lock. I was not a locksmith by any stretch of the imagination—the basic padlock on the supply cupboard was pretty much the extent of my skills, but lucky for me, Martin Smith had recently replaced his standard lock with a keyless pin pad that could be operated remotely. Something that I'd found out accidentally when I'd been going through the email records Weston had acquired, and had sparked the beginnings of a plan in my head.

Turning on my tiny key ring torch, I carefully swept it over the shiny keypad. Thanks to the surface, I could easily see the fingerprints over six of the numbers. I memorised them, then stepped back for a moment while I thought about the combination. These keypads gave three chances before you were automatically locked out of the system, and if I was unlucky, an alarm would also alert Martin Smith. So I had to act cautiously.

Fortunately, I liked a puzzle. Turning over the numbers in my head, I tried to line them up with what I knew about him. Most people when choosing a pin code would pick something that they'd easily remember—something mean-ingful, rather than a random string of numbers.

I immediately ruled out his date of birth since the numbers didn't fit, although it would have been too obvious of an option anyway. The only numbers that fitted, based on the information I had...it couldn't be, surely. Then again, it was clear that he hadn't had any contact with his ex-wife, so I was guessing their split hadn't been amicable.

Holding my breath, I typed in the date of his divorce and hit Enter.

24

lena

The light at the top of the keypad turned green, and I breathed a sigh of relief, slowly and carefully turning the door handle after pulling on a pair of latex gloves. Before I entered the apartment, I used the little antiseptic wipe I'd brought with me to go over the keypad quickly, although I doubted that my fingerprints would even be noticeable with the smeary prints that were already on there.

After that, I entered the hallway, closing the door softly behind me. Inside, everything was dark, which I was grateful for. Tiptoeing along the carpeted floor, I made my way towards the furthest room on the left. An easy search on a popular property website had brought up the floor plan of this place, so I knew the layout already.

My destination?

Martin Smith's bedroom.

Or more specifically, his phone.

There was a sudden yowl, and a ball of fur and claws launched itself at me.

Thinking fast, I spun away from the cat and opened the door to my right. The kitchen.

The cat flew through the door, and I spun again, yanking it shut, pausing at the last second so that it wouldn't slam. Easing it closed, I ignored the outraged hiss. Nothing was going to detract me from my purpose.

Inching along what felt like the world's longest hallway, I finally made it to the bedroom. The door was ajar, and I peered through it before even thinking about opening it any wider. Of course, the bedroom had to be pitch-black. I could barely make out anything.

Time to use my trusty torch. Pressing the little button to turn it on, I directed the beam into the palm of my hand, then carefully pointed the edge of the beam at the floor.

My heart was racing. I'd done stuff that other people would probably consider dangerous or ill-advised, but this...I'd never broken into someone's house before. Although, I guess there hadn't been any actual breaking in, since I'd used his passcode.

It was doubtful the police would see it that way, though.

As usual, I blocked those thoughts from my mind, allowing myself to become a shadow. My heart rate slowed, and my breathing became more even. Sweeping the torch across the floor, I took in the room at a glance. The lump in the bed that was a sleeping Martin Smith, the dresser against the far wall, a glint of metal...

There.

On the bedside table, next to a glasses case, was his phone.

Crouching down, I moved with agonising slowness, testing the floor in front of me with my toes before I dared to put my weight on it, hoping that the floorboards wouldn't creak and give away my presence. When I finally reached the bedside table, I waited for a moment, listening to his breathing and reassuring myself he was still asleep before I turned my attention to his phone.

It seemed to take forever as I inched it off the table and into my hands. My palms were sweaty, and the phone slipped before I managed to steady it against myself. Resting it on my knee, I eased open the zip pocket of my trousers and pulled out a tiny metal pin. I used the pin to pop open the slot on his phone that housed the SIM card and currently empty SD card slot. Taking out the little device I'd brought with me, I inserted it into the slot, then laid the phone back on the table. Hopefully he wouldn't notice it, or at least, not until it was too late.

His breath stuttered, and I reacted immediately, dropping flat to the floor.

Then he sat up in bed.

Fuck.

I did the only thing I could. I rolled under his bed.

The bed creaked, and then I heard a snapping sound which could have only been his glasses case opening. Holding my breath, I waited, feeling the mattress dip dangerously low so that it was almost touching my face.

Then his weight was gone, and I could breathe again. That was, until he flicked the bedside lamp on. I shuffled further into the shadows under the bed, trying not to panic by reminding myself that the odds of him actually looking under his bed were incredibly low. I mean, who looks under their bed every time they get up?

There was no way I was going to risk moving—the only way in and out of the apartment was through the front door, and I wasn't about to pull a Winter and risk broken legs or worse by climbing out of the window. Especially since we were right on the top floor. The only thing I could do was wait.

Finally, finally, he was in bed and asleep again, or at least, I hoped so. Rolling out from under the bed, I tiptoed towards the door.

Two more steps.

I made it to the hallway, and there was the front door. Almost out. Passing the kitchen, I noticed that the door that I'd closed was now ajar. I sensed it almost before I saw it, that ball of hissing, spitting fur coming for me.

There was a crash as I staggered into the small console table that stood against the wall.

Not bothering to take my time, I ran for it. I heard a shout from the hallway, but as I threw the front door closed behind me—as softly as I could in my hurry—I didn't see anyone, so I could only hope that Smith hadn't reached the door of his bedroom.

There was nowhere to hide on this floor, so I raced down the stairs as fast as I could, all while trying to avoid the cameras. By the time I'd reached the second floor, I heard the faint sound of a door opening above me, and I pushed myself even harder.

Instead of going out of the front door, where anyone looking out of their windows would see me, I aimed for the supply cupboard again. I hid there for what felt like hours, sitting on an upturned bucket, until I judged it was safe to leave.

Back in my bedroom at home, I turned on the computer program that would record Martin Smith's calls in real time. All I could do now was wait. There was a flashing icon on my screen, which meant that someone from Kryptos had left me a message.

My heart skipped a beat seeing the name Nitro appear. *Weston.*

Nitro: Cass wants you to stay home instead of intercepting the dogs exchange.
Me: No.

He was clearly online, because he replied straight away.

Nitro: He was adamant
Me: He needs to trust me. I know what I'm doing.
Nitro: I know, but you can be impulsive sometimes. He worries about you.
Me: Do YOU worry about me?
Nitro: What's that supposed to mean?
Me: You've been distancing yourself

There was no reply, but a few minutes later, my phone rang, and his name flashed up on the screen.

"Hi." His voice came down the line, all low and husky as if he was trying not to be overheard. My body's reaction was instant, and I frowned. I'd spent years loving Weston in secret, used to not acting on my feelings, and this sudden desire was so unexpected.

"Hi." I aimed for casual, but I was pretty sure that I didn't convince either of us. "What's up?"

He sighed into the phone. "You said I've been distancing myself."

"Yeah, because you have." Stepping away from the computer, I swiped my car keys from the desk and left my bedroom.

"I know," he eventually admitted, after a moment's silence. "It's...complicated."

"Talk to me. Please, West." Padding up the stairs to the upper floor, I pulled my phone away from my ear to check the time. I hadn't slept yet, having spent half the night inside Martin Smith's apartment building, but I was running high on adrenaline right now.

"Fuck, Lena. It's— It's... A lot of it is to do with your brother. He's my best friend."

"Don't you think I know that?" I snapped, then bit my lip. "Sorry, didn't mean it like that."

Another sigh. "Look, he asked if there was anything going on between us, and I lied to his face and said there wasn't. I can't lie to my best mate. It kills me."

"We need to talk. In person." I hit the button on my car key to unlock the door, then slid behind the wheel.

"I know we do," he admitted, and that was all I needed to hear. Without a reply, I hung up the phone and directed my car towards his house.

Once I'd arrived, I parked off to the side of the house and used the key I'd had cut recently to let myself in. It was more than likely that everyone was asleep by now— everyone other than Weston, hopefully. I needed to talk to him, to work out what was going on in his head. He'd find it much more difficult to avoid me in person, I'd make sure of it.

My first stop was the computer room, but the door was locked and there was no sound from inside. I didn't know the pin code, so instead, I turned around and headed up the stairs.

Straight for Weston's bedroom.

25

weston

Stepping out of the shower, I roughly ran the towel over my hair before wrapping it around my waist. The bathroom was steamy, too hot, almost, and I was glad to escape into my slightly cooler bedroom. As I closed the bathroom door behind me, I heard the unmistakable quiet click of my bedroom door opening.

What the fuck?

Who was sneaking into my room at this time of night?

The dim bedside lamp illuminated my answer. Her gaze flared with heat at the sight of me standing in nothing but a towel, water droplets still beading on my skin. It wasn't like I was expecting visitors. Her eyes licked a fiery trail over my body, and I flexed my muscles, earning me a small eye roll that couldn't dampen her heated gaze.

Since Lena was taking in every inch of my body, I returned the favour. I took my time running my gaze over her tight black leather-looking trousers that clung to her long legs, over her fitted black top, and up to her hair that spilled over her shoulders. Stopping on her face, I took in the curve of her lips and her darkening eyes as we stared at one another silently. When her eyes flicked down to the growing bulge that was obvious behind the material of my towel and she licked her lips, I'd had enough.

"Come here."

"Wait." She blinked a few times. "Let me...uh. I'm going to stay right here until we've talked."

"You want to talk?"

Her mouth twisted, but she nodded, lowering herself to the floor where she leaned her back against the wall.

"What do you want to talk about?" I asked cautiously, not really liking the look on her face.

She chewed on her lip for a moment, and then her eyes met mine. "I want to know why you've been avoiding me."

"It's...complicated," I offered, adjusting my towel. Crossing to my bed, I lay on top of the sheets on my side, facing her. May as well get comfortable if we were having this conversation.

"Then simplify it. What's the problem? I'm not interested in playing games." Her voice was hard, but her eyes... fuck, the vulnerability in them killed me.

"Your brother is my best friend. He's been there for me all my life, but particularly after my mum died and Cade shut himself away from me. I felt like I'd lost my brother, but Cass stepped in and...he's my closest friend, y'know?"

"I know that."

"Yeah, so I don't wanna hurt him. He's worried about you, and he more or less warned me off you."

She narrowed her eyes, unhappy. "He doesn't get a say in my life. He's got no right to make decisions for me. I'm eighteen, for fuck's sake."

"He's just trying to look out for you." I beckoned her

over to me, and this time she came, standing in one graceful movement. My head was reminding me that I'd literally just told her that I was worried about Cassius, but I wanted her. So fucking much.

But even without the issue of Cassius, I needed to take care.

I moved to the far side of the bed, allowing her plenty of space, and after a second's hesitation, she kicked off her boots and lay next to me, rolling to her side so we were facing each other.

"Is that the only problem?" She inched closer, placing her hand on my arm. A small smile curved across her lips as my breath caught in my throat.

She knew that the other reason I wanted to take things slowly was because of everything she'd been through, so I didn't reply. In fact, I did the most stupid thing I could've done.

I kissed her.

It turned out that it was easy enough to silence my doubts when the girl I wanted was right there in front of me.

Her lips parted for me instantly, her hand sliding up my arm to cup the back of my neck as I deepened the kiss. I dragged her closer, palming her ass, and she moaned low in her throat. "Is this okay?" My mouth disconnected from hers, and I placed kisses down her throat, my body pressing into hers.

I caught the moment she stiffened, and I immediately pulled back. She stared up at me. "I'm sorry. It's just…"

"It's okay." Gripping her tightly, I rolled us both so she was on top of me and held her lightly until she relaxed again. After a minute she sat up, her body weight resting on my stomach. Then she wriggled backwards, and I couldn't stop the groan that came from my throat.

"Fuck, yes."

She rolled her hips against my hardness. "I think I like this view." All I could do was watch, my eyes tracking her every movement, my dick throbbing as she ran her palms down over my chest, pausing to trace the outline of my Roman numerals IV tattoo, down my abs, then onto her own body.

"It's hot in here, isn't it?" Her tone was low and throaty.

"What?" I asked, dazed.

A slow smile appeared on her lips as she dragged her top up over her body.

Oh, fuck.

She didn't have a bra on, and as her firm, high tits came into view, it took every single shred of self-control I possessed not to reach up and drag her down, rip off her trousers, and bury myself inside her. My fists clenched and unclenched. Just a touch. My hands came up to her sides, stroking across her smooth skin.

"You feel so good, Lena."

"I'm going to feel a whole lot better soon," she promised me, and all I could do was stare at her.

"I wasn't expecting this."

She gave me a look that was almost pitying. "Oh, Weston. Just because I never found anyone that I was interested in doing this with before—" Yeah, no fucking pressure. "—doesn't mean that I don't know what I'm doing." Her words faltered for a minute, before her confidence returned. "We both want this, and I know you'll tell me if I do anything you don't like."

"I like it all," I said hoarsely, and she laughed.

"I think you'll like it better in a minute." Lifting her body off me for a moment, she shimmied out of her leggings at my side, then took a moment to take me in, lying there ready for her. Reaching out her hand, she ran it over the top of my towel, over my cock.

"Lena, *fuck*." My cock jerked under her hand.

Releasing me, she laid her body across mine, burying her face in my shoulder, all her silky-smooth skin against me.

"Can I touch you?" I whispered.

"*Please*."

I didn't need to hear any more. This girl was mine. And I was going to make her mine in every sense of the word. Running my hands down her back, I captured her lips in a kiss that started off slow but dialled up to a hundred in the space of about five seconds. "West, please," she whimpered, rocking her hips against me as my hands slid over every inch of her skin. Her hand went between us, tugging at my towel.

I managed to regain enough brain function to still her hand. "Wait."

Her head came up, and she stared at me, confused.

"Do you trust me?" I held her gaze, waiting until she nodded. "Lie down on your back."

She immediately obeyed, and I took a moment to appreciate the thought that the headstrong, wilful Lena was so willing to comply with me in my bed.

"Remember, if you ever feel uncomfortable, tell me to stop and I will."

Splayed out below me, her pink hair all tousled and her body flushed, she was beautiful. Ignoring my aching dick was easier than I expected when my full focus was on her pleasure. I wanted to make her moan and cry for me, to fall apart under my touch.

"You're so fucking beautiful," I murmured, holding myself over her, using my arms to keep my body weight off her. Pushing her hair back from her face, I placed a kiss to her temple, then kissed down the side of her face, pausing at her jaw. I hovered over her mouth, and her lips parted on a sigh as I closed the distance, teasing her bottom lip lightly with my teeth before releasing it. She huffed as I moved out of reach of her mouth, and I laughed against her before kissing the hollow of her throat.

"Good?" I adjusted my position, my mouth moving down to her collarbone while my hand went to her breast, circling around her nipple but not touching it.

"Torturer," she moaned, arching upwards, trying to push against my hand.

Lifting my head, I took in her dilated pupils as she watched everything I was doing with wide eyes. "Hmm...do you like this?" I lowered my head and took her nipple into my mouth, tugging it between my teeth, then swirling my tongue around it.

"Ohhhh..." was the only noise that came from her, her back arching off the bed, and I moved to her other breast, teasing and touching her with my hand and mouth until she was panting beneath me.

Shifting again on the bed, I moved lower, down her smooth stomach, dropping kisses while my hand ran over her sides and down over her legs. When I reached her underwear, I stopped, glancing up at her to make sure she was okay. Other than her chest rising and falling with her rapid breathing, she remained still, waiting to see what I was going to do next.

I didn't keep her waiting long.

I took the band of her underwear between my teeth and tugged it down.

A shocked gasp escaped her, but she caught on quickly, lifting her hips so I could use my teeth to slide the fabric free from her body. When she was completely bare, she instinctively tried to close her legs, but I kept her thighs apart as I met her eyes again.

"Legs wider," I instructed, running my hands over her thighs, reassuring her with my actions. She let me manoeuvre her into position, and then I lowered my head.

A tiny moan fell from her lips as I blew across her pussy, so fucking wet that I wanted to slide my dick in more than anything I'd ever wanted before. But that could wait. Nothing else was happening until she'd come for me.

I dragged my tongue through her wetness, and she arched off the bed with a cry.

Reaching up, I placed a finger to my lips, and she sighed against me, staring down at me with darkened eyes. I doubted the others would hear us since I had a bathroom between my room and the next, but better to be on the safe side.

Dipping my head again, I licked her, taking my time, and when she was writhing below me, I sucked her clit into my mouth.

"Fucking *fuck*, Weston!" Her cry tore from her throat, and I brought my fingers up, pumping in and out of her soaked pussy while I licked and sucked at her clit. Her thigh stiffened under my hand, and I increased the pressure until she shuddered around me, clamping down on my head with her thighs. Withdrawing my fingers, I licked her slowly until her hands came down to tug at my hair.

Her body trembled under me, and I released my grip on her thighs. "Enough. I can't...it's too sensitive." Her voice was completely breathless, and when I met her eyes, she had a glazed, blissed-out look in them.

I'd done that.

Making Lena Drummond fall apart might just be my new favourite thing.

26

lena

My brain eventually came back online, and I became aware of Weston, now lying next to me, his head on the pillow as he lazily traced his fingers up and down my arm. I turned my head. "Hi."

He smiled, all slow and satisfied, and I couldn't even muster up a glare at his smugness. He had every right to be satisfied after what he'd done to me.

"Okay. First of all, we're doing that again."

His smile widened at my words, and he moved incrementally closer. "That can be arranged."

"Second of all." I closed the last bit of space between us and spoke against his lips. "We're doing that again." Then I kissed his grinning face, because I couldn't resist him. His smile curved against my mouth before he kissed me back, pulling me on top of him.

"Do you think you're ready for more?" His voice was low and sexy as fuck, and as he spoke, he gripped my ass, pressing me against his hard cock.

"Why do you still have this on?" Sitting up, I stared pointedly down at his towel, riding low on his hips, or more accurately, the prominent outline of his dick. Without waiting for a reply, I gripped the fabric and tugged it away from him, allowing his hardness to spring free. He made a kind of growling sound that made me shiver, as he tracked my movements through darkened eyes.

Lowering myself back on top of him, I hesitated for a moment. His hands came to my hips.

"Do you want to lie on your back?"

I shook my head. I didn't want there to be any chance of me freaking out, not when I was finally about to get Weston Cavendish. I'd never thought I'd be here in this place, with his strong, tattooed body under mine, his hands on me, wanting *me*. Whatever reservations he'd had were long gone, and I wanted this. *Him*. So, so much.

Understanding flashed in his eyes, and he pulled me down to him. "Kiss me." I lost myself in his kisses, his touch, the feel of his body against mine. His hand snaked down between us. "So fucking wet for me." His breath was hot and heavy against my ear. "Are you ready for my cock now?"

"*Yes*."

Pulling me up so he could meet my eyes, he stared at me for a minute, more serious than I'd ever seen him. "This is your first time, right?"

"Yeah," I whispered. "There was never anyone else that caught my interest. No one other than you."

Fuck. Why was I telling him this? Was he about to run for the hills?

His eyes flashed with a kind of possessive pleasure, sending bolts of lust straight to my core. "Are you on the pill?"

I nodded. I had been for a couple of years now as a way to regulate my cycle.

"Okay." He swallowed hard, watching me through lowered lids. "I…I've been tested, and I'm all good. I want —" Pausing again, he licked his lips, his hand coming up to cup my face. He stroked his thumb across my cheekbone as he continued. "I want to give you one of my firsts, too."

"What do you mean?" I hardly dared to breathe.

"I want you with nothing between us. No condom."

A whimper fell from my lips, and I buried my face in his shoulder, my heart racing. "I want that, too." I hoped he understood the garbled words I mumbled against his skin. Was it silly to feel so overcome? It felt like he was giving me a gift. It felt like it meant something to him. Something more than just sex. Or maybe that was just me projecting.

But his words lit me up inside.

"Good." His voice was soft, and the slight tremor I heard reassured me even further. Lifting my head, I kissed him before sitting up. He ran his hands down my thighs. "There should be a bottle of lube in the bedside drawer. It'll make things easier for you."

When I had it in hand, I looked down at him, unsure for a minute. He smiled. "Want me to—"

"I think I can work out what to do with this." I warmed the lube in my hands, then reached down to his cock. Wrapping both my hands around him, I stroked him up and down in a twisting motion.

"Fuck…" he groaned, his head falling back as he thrust his hips upwards. "Where did…fuck…where did you learn all this?"

"There's an amazing invention called Google."

He laughed, before groaning again as I palmed the head of his dick, the precum combining with the lube, all hot and slick in my grip.

"I should do myself, too, right?" Coating my fingers in more of the slippery lube, I reached down between my legs.

"Fucking hell." Weston raised himself up on his elbows, tracking every movement of my fingers, his breath coming in short pants. "That's...you're so fucking hot."

"I need you." I was so wet and ready for him, needed him inside me.

I fucking *ached* for him.

Sliding forwards, I ground myself along the length of his dick. Then again. "Fuck. This feels so good," I moaned. "West. I need..."

"I know, baby." His hands came to my hips. "Lift up. Try to relax, okay?"

Rising up onto my knees, I let him guide me with one hand, while his other gripped his cock, lining it up. He kept up his murmured instructions, taking his time and making sure I was okay. Then his head was at my entrance, and he was pushing inside.

He was *so* big. The burn and the stretch as I sank down onto him, impossibly full, was like nothing I'd ever imagined.

"Don't move," he panted. "You feel...fuck. Being bare inside you..." He threw his hand over his face, clearly struggling to regain control.

There was no way I could move right now, anyway.

He raised himself into a seated position, and our lips met. His hands tangled in my hair as our bodies pressed together. Was his heart thumping as loudly as mine? My body was overloaded with sensations.

I wanted to move.

I needed to move.

Gripping onto him, I rolled my hips in a small, slow movement.

Oh, yes.

"*Lena*." He reached down between us, his fingers finding my clit.

"Don't stop." I gasped as he chased away the pain with new sensations, sending pulses of pleasure through my entire body. Rocking against him again, I held on to him more tightly, my nails digging into his skin as I rode him.

My movements sped up, his hips meeting mine, both of us chasing the high that was building between us.

"I can't hold on." His voice was ragged. "Fuck, I can't—" He pressed down on my clit as his whole body tensed up, his cock pulsing inside me, filling me with his cum.

It sent me over the edge.

My orgasm burned through me, hot and all-consuming. My head fell forwards to rest against his as I let myself go, knowing that he'd catch me when I fell.

I came back to reality to find his hands stroking through my hair, his forehead resting against mine as our breathing finally began to slow. "You doing okay?" He pulled back a bit so he could see me.

"Yeah," I whispered. I couldn't form any more words, but it was enough. He gave me one of those slow, lazy smiles, and my stomach flipped.

"Good. This might be a bit painful." Carefully holding me, he lifted me off him, which made me wince. No doubt about it, I'd still be feeling this tomorrow.

So worth it.

"Stay there." He guided me down onto my back. I lay there, eyes closed, deliciously sated and sore. The sounds of him moving around, followed by a running tap, had me blinking my eyes open to watch him reappear in the bathroom doorway. He crossed the room to the bed and gently ran a soft washcloth over me. His eyes darkened as he stared down between my legs. "My cum dripping out of you..." His eyes closed for a second, and then his gaze met mine. "*My* cum. *You*."

I smiled at the combination of possessiveness and wonder in his expression and tone. "Yeah, you did that with your giant dick."

He snorted, humour flashing in his gaze, before he turned serious again. "Did I hurt you?"

"No." I shook my head. There had been pain, sure, but way less than I'd imagined, despite the sheer size of him. He'd made it as painless as possible for me, and it made me fall even harder. "I'll be feeling it tomorrow, but..." Trailing off, I reached my arms up, and he came to me, crawling over my body and staring down into my eyes. "I want to do that again."

"We will." His lips met mine, and he kissed me, all slow and languid, and I melted beneath him. He spoke against my lips. "Now I've had you, I want more. Just so you know."

I laughed tiredly, but his words generated a spark inside me. "I'm down for that."

I hoped he didn't want to stop. I hoped he meant those words. I'd fallen too far, too hard, and he had the power to ruin me, now. I could only hope and pray that he would fall, too, so I wasn't alone in this. I wanted to own his heart, not just his body. I wanted all of him.

"Good." Rolling off me, he lay on his back and tugged me into his side, then tucked the duvet around us. "Sleep now."

My eyes closed, and I let sleep pull me under, held by the boy I loved.

27

weston

I n the cold light of day, I had time to think. Lena slept soundly next to me, her body curled up under the covers and her hair fanned out over the pillow. Last night had been...intense. I'd never fucked anyone without a condom before—never even wanted to.

The guilt I'd been suppressing raged through me again. How could I look Cassius in the eye now? I'd been doing okay, keeping her at a distance, and then last night had happened.

I needed to put distance between us.

Next to me, she stirred, her eyes blinking open sleepily. "What time is it?"

"Almost nine." As I looked down at her, the guilt I'd been feeling only a few seconds ago disappeared. Why would I want to put any distance between us?

She placed a soft, tentative kiss to my chest, right on my IV tattoo, and my heart beat faster. I tugged her on top of me, loving this soft, sleepy version of my girl.

What the fuck, Weston?

Great, now I was fucking talking to myself.

A knock at my bedroom door had Lena scrambling off me with a screech and diving under the covers.

"Yeah?" I called, trying not to laugh.

"We're out of coffee, so I'm going to do a coffee run. Want anything?" Winter's voice came through my door, and I relaxed. She wouldn't invade my privacy by barging in here. I was fairly sure the door was locked, anyway.

"Yeah. Can you get me a latte?" I paused. "And a mocha?"

"*Oh*."

I groaned because I knew that Winter had figured it out. There was silence for a minute, before she spoke again. "Got it. Don't make me keep another secret, please."

Sliding out of the bed, I padded across the floor and opened my door a crack. "I won't. Just give me a bit of time, yeah? I don't wanna fuck things up. For either of them."

She nodded slowly. "Okay. I don't envy your situation, by the way."

"Thanks," I said dryly.

"You're welcome. Cade's coming with me by the way, and Cass isn't here. So you don't need to worry about running into them. Just...please don't leave it too long. Secrets have a way of fucking us over, even if we think we're doing the right thing by keeping them."

I scrubbed my hand across my face, keeping my voice low. "I know. It's complicated. I never planned on any of this."

"I know you didn't, and I know you need time to get your head around it." Her voice softened. "I'm here if you want to talk to me, you know that. Either of you."

"I know."

With a small smile, she backed away, pulling the door closed behind her. When I turned around, Lena was sitting up in the bed, watching me with an unreadable expression on her face.

"Did you hear that?" There was no point in asking her, because it was clear that she had. I sighed. "I don't know what to do here."

Instead of replying, she nodded.

"Lena, look—" My words were interrupted by another soft knock at the door, and this time, Winter poked her head around it.

"I thought Lena might want to borrow some clothes." She handed me a bundle of fabric and peered over my shoulder to smile at Lena.

"Thanks." That was the only word Lena spoke, and then as soon as Winter was gone, she was out of the bed and taking the clothes from my arms. She disappeared into the bathroom, and I heard the lock click behind her.

Probably for the best. We both needed space to think.

When I returned to my bedroom after showering in the guest bathroom, Lena had disappeared, so I headed downstairs to the kitchen.

I stopped dead in the doorway.

Lena was in the kitchen, seated at the island, and she wasn't alone.

Next to her, his arm brushing against hers, his tatted torso on shameless display, was Zayde.

That jealous knot twisted inside me as she inclined her head closer to his, smiling. When he gently gripped her wrist, flipping it over and dragging his finger across her skin, I couldn't watch anymore. I moved backwards to leave the room but knocked into the door with my heel. It didn't make much noise, but it was enough to alert them to the fact I was there. Both of them spun around, Zayde dropping Lena's wrist, and Lena flushing guiltily.

"What's going on here?" My words were clipped as I spoke through clenched teeth.

"What does it look like?" Zayde raised a brow, completely cool and unaffected as always.

"I don't know, that's why I was asking," I gritted out.

"Nothing's going on." There was still a flush to Lena's cheeks, and I didn't believe her for one minute.

"Right." Swallowing down the ball of hurt that had lodged itself in my throat, I took another step backwards. "Got to check something in the computer room." Then I turned and escaped, because I couldn't stay there with them any longer.

Locking the door behind me, I sank into the large leather chair in front of my monitors, refusing to think about what I'd just seen. It could be innocent, but the way he'd been touching her, and the look on her face when she'd seen me—those weren't the actions of people who had nothing to hide.

And I'd slept with her last night. What if it was all a game to her?

I shook my head, annoyed at myself. I was thinking irrationally now. I needed to stay in here, cool off, and maybe I could face whatever it was with a clear head. Normally if I had a problem, I'd go to Cassius or my brother —both of them weren't options right now because they were too close to the people involved, and as for Winter...it wasn't fair to keep involving her in a situation where she was forced to take sides or keep secrets. I knew how much it cut her up, and I couldn't keep doing it to her.

None of my other friends were close enough for me to confide in, not even Rumi, who I'd been friends with for years. This was the kind of shit that I could only talk about with the people that I trusted implicitly.

There was only one person left I could speak to. And if I spoke to him, I'd have to tell him my other secret.

I remained still, rolling my thoughts over and over in my mind.

Then, I took my phone from my pocket and called my dad.

"Weston." My dad inclined his head in greeting as one of his security showed me into his home office. He hadn't got around to replacing Allan, our long-time butler, after everything that had happened. I suspected that he didn't want to —didn't trust anyone enough to let them in again. Allan's involvement in Christine's betrayal had affected us all, but my dad had relied on him for so much. Even though Allan had saved my dad's life before he died, taking a bullet for him, it didn't negate the way that he'd been working against us for so long with Christine.

Shaking off those negative thoughts, because my current problems were enough to deal with at this point in time, I took a seat in a slightly uncomfortable high-backed tan leather chair to the right of his desk.

"Tea? Coffee? I was just about to have one."

I nodded, and he swiped the screen of his phone, presumably sending our orders to the kitchen staff via the app I had developed for him last year. Once he was done with that, he sat back in his chair, studying me thoughtfully.

"I need," I began, clearing my throat. "I need your advice."

Shock flared in his eyes, which he quickly masked, and then a small smile tugged at the corners of his mouth. "I wasn't expecting that," he said honestly. A silver fountain pen lay on his desk, and he picked it up, turning it over in his hands as he waited for me to continue.

"Yeah, well…" I shrugged. My voice sounded quiet and sad, even to my own ears. "I don't have anyone else to talk to."

Concern filled his gaze, and he stood, glancing down at me. "We need to be more comfortable for this conversation. Let's reconvene in the den—I'll get our coffees. Will we be needing a brandy or two for this?"

Despite myself, I smiled. "Maybe. Probably. Or at least, you will."

He nodded briskly. "Right. Den."

Seated in the small den on one of the squashy sofas, I waited for my dad to return. A few minutes later, he appeared in the doorway with a tray with two steaming cups of coffee. Placing the tray on the coffee table, he headed over to the sideboard and took a bottle and two glasses before returning to me. Once he was seated and had poured us each a generous finger of brandy, I began.

My voice grew hoarse as I told him everything. Everything barring Lena's assault, because that wasn't my information to share. Instead, I mentioned that there had been an incident that had affected her, but I was sure he could read between the lines. He didn't seem surprised, either, which made me think that he knew more than I had originally thought.

When I'd finally finished, my face hot because even though I hadn't given him details, even telling him I'd slept with a girl made me cringe, he took a sip of his brandy, rubbing his thumb over the glass.

"Okay. This is a lot to take in, son. Before we go through

the things you've told me, I want to mention your side business, which I have to say, has rather taken me aback."

"Kryptos? Me being Nitro?"

He nodded. "Maybe I was wilfully ignorant, but I never made the connection between Nitro and my son." An appreciative smile spread across his face. "I'm proud of you, Weston."

His words healed something inside me that I wasn't even aware was broken. "Thank you." My voice cracked, and I attempted to disguise it by clearing my throat, then leaning forwards to pick up my drink.

"Now, I'm not condoning illegal activities, of course. But sometimes my memory can be...let's say...selective." His smile morphed into a smirk, his eyes dancing in the morning light that poured through the tall windows.

My own mouth turned up, as I relaxed back against the sofa. "Yeah, just like I don't remember what happened at the docks with the explosion."

"Docks? Explosion? I'm afraid I don't know what you're referring to."

"Exactly." We grinned at each other, and in that moment, I felt closer to him than I ever had before.

Placing his drink back down, he eyed me carefully. "As for the rest of it. I'm not the best person to ask for relationship advice. But I want you to remember this. Everyone has their own problems, Weston. Now, they're not always noticeable on the surface." He blew out a heavy breath. "But I want you to remember that sometimes those you think are the strongest are the ones barely holding it together. You may envy them, think that they have their life sorted out, and you wonder what they have that you don't. What you don't see is the moment when they're alone and their mask slips, and they fall apart with no one to hold them up." His voice grew hoarse as he finished speaking, and his eyes glistened suspiciously.

"Dad?"

"Sorry." He cleared his throat. "I don't—I— My point was, that no one is perfect. No relationship is perfect. You've seen this with Lena. She comes across as strong and confident, sometimes even hard, at times, but I have the feeling you've only scratched the surface of who she is inside. She needs someone to lean on, to be there for her. Can you be that person? Only time will tell, but from what you've told me, it sounds like she has strong feelings for you. Now, I haven't seen you together, but let's call it a gut instinct—if what you've told me is correct, then I don't think you have a reason to worry about Zayde. Why would she jeopardise that?"

"Hmm." I stared into my glass as if it could provide all the answers. "What about Zayde, though?"

"Does Zayde know that you're involved with Lena?"

"No." Taking a sip of the brandy, I grimaced. Placing it back down, I switched it with my coffee, taking a large gulp to chase away the burn of the alcohol.

"Zayde keeps himself to himself, we know this. He's always been hard to read, even when he was younger." My dad tapped his fingers on the arm of the sofa, thinking. "But he's loyal, and he's a good friend. I'm positive that if you went to him with your concerns, he wouldn't hesitate to reassure you."

"Maybe." I eyed him doubtfully.

"Just talk to him. These days, I'm a big fan of talking things out, thanks to Winter."

"I guess." Tipping my coffee to my lips, I took another gulp. "What about the rest of it?"

He leaned forwards on the sofa. "How important is

Lena to you? Could you let her go? If the answer is no, then you need to talk to Cassius. It's not fair to keep this from him. If the answer is yes, then you need to break things off now, for both of your sakes."

My mouth twisted. He was right, of course.

"What about the Martin Smith thing?"

His expression lightened. "I trust that you'll figure it out. Just promise me that you won't go getting yourself into any more dangerous situations."

"We're dealing with possible dog fighting and shady deals here, not psychos," I reminded him.

"Weston, please. Stay safe. I couldn't handle anything happening to you."

"I'll do my best."

He gave a heavy sigh. "I guess that's all I can ask for."

Back in my car, I sat for a while, turning his words over in my head.

How important was Lena to me, and what would happen to Cassius' and my friendship if we were together?

And what the fuck was going on with her and Zayde?

28

weston

As I walked back into the house, my steps slowed. I headed towards the kitchen, when my arm was grabbed and I was roughly tugged backwards, back in the direction of the front door.

"What the fuck?" I managed to say, before Zayde was handing me a helmet and indicating for me to follow him outside. It didn't even occur to me to question what he was doing or where we were going—he'd never voluntarily gone anywhere with me on his bike before. We were all close friends, sure, but he always held a part of himself back, keeping a wall between himself and the rest of the world. A wall that only my brother had really been able to penetrate. And maybe Winter. I knew he had a bit of a soft spot for her.

Minutes later we were heading down the coastal road, his powerful motorbike roaring beneath us. I kept a tight grip on the grab rail, watching the scenery fly by, almost too fast to take in. He turned onto another road, then another, then another, and eventually he slowed right down, cruising along a road of modern, Scandinavian-style houses made from wood with huge glass windows, sprawling on either side of the road. He came to a stop at the very end of the road, just past the final house, where there was a series of large ponds surrounded by bullrushes, with a clump of trees behind them.

He removed his helmet, and his icy eyes met mine, his expression giving nothing away. Curious, I removed my own helmet and followed him down to the ponds. He stopped next to the trees that backed the pond on our right, sprawling out and resting his elbows on the grass. The sun was bright, but here under the shade of the trees, it was dim and cool.

"There was a girl," he began, then stopped. His tone turned low and threatening as he levelled me with one of his signature looks. "What I'm telling you now is confidential."

"Can you not use your serial killer voice, please?" I was only half-joking.

He made a noise that sounded a lot like a growl, making me roll my eyes. "First Winter tells me I have a serial killer stare, now you say I have a serial killer voice. What the fuck?"

Since it was clear he was talking to himself, I ignored that question as I lowered myself to the grass, reclining back on my own elbows.

"There was a girl," he said again, his expression completely blank. "We were...close. I used to come here with her, sometimes."

I just stared at him, unable to comprehend a world in which Zayde even had a girl he was close to, let alone one that he'd bring anywhere like this.

"She reminded me of Lena, in a way. Not..." I waited while he gathered his thoughts. His fingers shredded an unsuspecting flower while I waited for him to continue, ripping it into tiny pieces that were carried away on the breeze. "Not much, really, but she had a wild streak to her. And blonde hair. Like a fucking angel." His voice grew quieter as he lost himself in his memories.

He paused for a moment, then raised his eyes to mine. "I saw your face when you saw me with Lena in the kitchen this morning. And the other times, too."

"Sooo..." I prompted, when the silence stretched uncomfortably.

"When we were at that party and I gave Lena a ride home..."

My stomach churned.

"At that moment, there was something that made me remember. I wanted—" He stopped talking but dropped his mask for a second, and I could read him.

"You wanted to remember? You wanted a piece of her?"

He nodded slowly. "It wasn't fair. No one could take her place." He tipped his head back, staring up at the branches of the tree. "Nothing happened with Lena. It wouldn't have even if I hadn't come to that decision. She wanted you."

"Why did she go home with you, then?" I couldn't disguise the hurt in my voice, no matter if it was irrational or not.

"Ask her" was all he said.

Pushing myself up into a sitting position, I waited until his eyes returned to mine. "What happened to the girl?"

There was a brief flash of pain in his eyes, so raw and powerful that my jaw dropped. He masked it so quickly that I wondered if I'd imagined it.

"She's not around anymore."

His tone was final, and I took the hint. Instead, I voiced the question that I wasn't sure I wanted the answer to.

"What about this morning?"

"What about it? What was it you think you saw?"

Plucking at the blades of grass between my fingers, I watched him carefully. "I think I saw two people who had something to hide." He opened his mouth, but I continued. Fuck it. My dad was right. Might as well talk it out, even though talking to Zayde was as useful as talking to a brick wall sometimes. "I *hope* that it was just my imagination."

"Do you really think I'd fuck around with your girl?" His tone was flat and impossible to read.

I went with the truth.

"No. But she's not my girl."

"Isn't she?" He raised his brow. "Want to bet on that?"

"Not really."

We lapsed into silence after that, but for some reason it wasn't weird. I watched the dragonflies darting around the pond, gradually relaxing. Across from me, Zayde's eyes catalogued everything around us, his gaze constantly on the move, until he paused on a tree behind the central lake. He sucked in a harsh breath, and before I could do or say anything, he got to his feet and disappeared.

A couple of minutes later, he reappeared between the trees, and he ran his hand over the bark of the tree that he'd been so intent on when he was sitting with me.

My head was fucking spinning. It felt like this moment was significant for him, somehow, and yet he'd shared it with me. I didn't know what was going on with him, and I knew he wouldn't tell me. One thing I was sure of now, though, deep down, was that he didn't have any interest in Lena.

He finally headed back to me, unreadable as always, but there was a heaviness to him that hadn't been there when we'd arrived. We stayed by the ponds for a long time, sharing a joint, not talking, just soaking up the quiet. Long enough that my phone started lighting up with texts asking where I was.

Presumably Z had had the same texts, because he suddenly stood, and without a word, picked up his helmet.

Once we were back at the house, he turned to me after removing his helmet. "Don't let your issues cloud your judgement" was all he said before he disappeared.

Okay then.

I headed inside to face the music.

29

lena

Weston had been gone for most of the day. Ever since he'd seen me with Zayde in the kitchen, I'd had a sick feeling in my stomach that wouldn't go away. I was so fucking in love with Weston Cavendish, and I didn't want to do anything to jeopardise that. I knew he didn't feel the same way as me, but from the devastated expression on his face when he'd seen me with Zayde this morning, he had feelings for me.

Truthfully, I already knew that. The way he'd been with me last night blew me away. He'd made me feel special, cherished, and that was something that no one outside my family had ever been able to do.

When he walked back inside with Zayde, my stomach flipped. It took everything I had not to go to him, to drag him out of the room, to prove to him that he was the only one I wanted. The only one I'd ever wanted.

But everyone was in the lounge with me. Winter was on the sofa, curled up on Caiden's lap, and my brother was in an armchair. We'd been playing a game on the Xbox before

Weston and Zayde walked in, but the moment they'd appeared, it had been forgotten.

So I did the one thing that in hindsight probably wasn't the best idea.

I opened my mouth and told them what I'd done last night.

"Martin Smith."

Everyone turned to look at me.

"I was in his flat last night."

After I'd said the words, dead silence fell in the room. I sat up straight, defiance in my eyes, waiting for the judgements to rain down on me.

"Explain yourself." The first person to speak was Cassius, and he wasn't happy. I chanced a glance at West before I replied, and he was staring at me with blazing eyes. Anger, hurt, concern, lust...how did all of those things coexist in one person at the same time? It made me falter for a moment, and with effort, I tore my gaze from his and focused on my brother.

As I explained what had happened, the room fell silent again, disapproval and worry heavy in the air. It was stifling.

"I need a break." Before anyone could say anything, I rose to my feet and got the fuck out of there. I ran blindly through the hallway and into the kitchen, yanking open the doors and stepping outside onto the deck. Fresh air filled my lungs, and I inhaled deeply.

Everything was out of control.

I knew it had been a stupid idea to go there on my own, but no one would have agreed. Now, the entire house was pissed off with me, and for good reason. Even though I hadn't been caught, and even though the chip I'd added to Martin Smith's phone could lead to the breakthrough we needed, I knew that everyone saw me as reckless, making decisions without thinking through the consequences.

I made it a point to breathe in and out slowly and evenly, gripping the rail at the side of the deck to ground me. Eventually, my breathing slowed naturally, and I stared out across the grass, watching the last rays of the setting sun touch the edges of the garden, turning everything a burnished gold colour.

There was a small sound behind me.

Spinning, I sensed the presence before I even saw him. This time, even though he was angry, there was no panic. I knew I could fight if I wanted to, but I chose to let him pin me against the side of the house. Was it fucked up that I needed this? Needed *him*.

"We need to talk, Lena." His leg wedged between mine as he gripped my wrists. Even in the midst of his anger and hurt, he held me lightly, giving me the opportunity to break away from him.

The thing was? I didn't want to break away from him.

How could I, when he was all I saw?

"I'm so fucking angry at you for putting yourself in danger." He nipped at my throat.

Almost of their own volition, my hands went to his back, sliding down to his ass. I pulled him closer to me, and he responded by dipping his head to my neck, trailing kisses up my neck while his cock hardened against my thigh.

"Weston." That was all I needed to say, and then his lips found mine, kissing me like he needed me to breathe. I melted against him. He burned all my hard edges away, all my defences, leaving me exposed to him.

"We need to talk," he said roughly when we broke apart, both breathing heavily.

"The thing you saw this morning with Z," I rushed to explain, knowing that it was the source of his anger and hurt, rather than the fact I'd gone off alone. "Please believe me when I say that there was nothing there. I feel nothing for Zayde."

He drew back to look at me with a conflicted expression. "What about the time you went home with him?"

I instantly knew what he was referring to—the party where I'd chosen Zayde to take me home, even though West had offered first.

I met his eyes, willing him to believe me. "I was trying to make you jealous. I wanted you to notice me." My hands cupped the back of his neck, pulling him closer. "Don't you see it?" My voice faltered, but I pushed past it. I had to get the words out. "All I want is you."

He was silent for so long that a ball of dread lodged itself in my throat.

But when his words came, they were everything.

"I don't know when or how it happened." His hand caressed my face, brushing my hair back so he could see me properly. "You've flown under my radar for so long. But now..." He moved closer, his lips skating over mine. "Now, you're all I see."

Our lips met in the most explosive kiss yet, sparks of sensation flying through my entire body, his hands all over me, as I—

"*What the fuck is going on here?*"

Fuck, fuck, *fuck*.

30

weston

I ripped myself away from Lena, stumbling and steadying myself on the railing, but it was too late. Cassius was staring at us both, and the hurt in his eyes fucking killed me.

"Cass—" I started.

He held up his hand. "I don't want to hear it." His voice was low and cutting, like I'd never heard it before. "Save me the lies. You already lied to me when you told me nothing was going on between you and my sister." His voice rose. "What the fuck, West? You know what she's been through! Not to mention all of this shit that's happening now!"

"Wait a minute!" Lena was suddenly in his face, all angry, baring her teeth and her eyes flashing dangerously.

Wrong time for my dick to get hard. But fuck, she was hot like this.

"Don't even bother trying to defend yourself." He drew himself up to his full height, his blue eyes dark and stormy. "You have no justification for this."

"Stop being such a stubborn dickhead!" she shouted,

and he spun around, his fist slamming into the wall of the house.

Both Lena's and my mouths fell open as we watched the happiest, most generous and fun-loving person we'd ever known fall apart in a rage.

We'd done this.

No. *I'd* done this. If I'd been honest when he'd asked me about Lena, we wouldn't be in this situation right now.

"Cass?"

"No!" he roared, and then he was gone, the glass rattling in his wake as he slammed the sliding door shut with all his force.

The guilt choked me, making it hard to breathe. It became suffocating when I looked over at Lena to see silent tears running down her face.

"He's never—" she choked out, and I pulled her into my arms, letting her tears soak through my T-shirt and onto my skin as she shook against me. Seeing Cassius fall apart and now Lena crying?

How was I meant to handle this?

What was I supposed to do?

Against my will, tears obscured my vision, and I blinked hard, forcing them back.

This was all my fucking fault.

"Don't you dare." Lena's face was suddenly in front of mine. She swiped her own tears away impatiently. "Don't you dare blame yourself for this."

"It's my fault, though." I ran my hands up and down her back, still needing to touch her.

"You're not the only person in this," she reminded me softly. "I know he's your best friend, but he's my brother. Let me talk to him first."

Taking her hand, I led her over to the outdoor chairs

and pulled her down next to me. "Before that?" I met her tearstained gaze. "We need to talk about us."

She took in a deep, shuddering breath, then nodded.

"Okay."

When she was in my arms like this, everything was clear. I lifted her into my lap, and she rested her head against my shoulder. I spoke first. This was the first time I'd ever had a conversation like this with a girl, and it was easier now she wasn't looking at me.

"I like you." My arms wrapped around her. "I want to see where things go. I know I said it before, but I want you to know that I mean it. But we have a problem now."

"I know." She sighed against me.

"Let me talk to Cass. I was the one who fucked up—I should have been honest with him in the first place. He didn't deserve to find out this way."

"Okay. What are you going to say to him?"

"I don't know yet. But I think if I give him a bit of time to cool off, he'll be okay. I fucking hope so. I don't want to lose my best mate."

"And I don't want to lose my brother." Lifting her head, she twisted to face me. "I can't believe I'm saying this," she muttered. "But maybe it's best if we cool things off for now. I don't want to be flaunting it in front of him."

Her words cut me, but she was right. We owed it to Cassius. But I still found myself trying to work out a compromise in my head, a way that I got to keep both my girl and my best friend. "What do you mean? We already said we'd keep it friendly in public."

"I know. But I don't think I can do that anymore." Her lashes lowered, and she murmured her next words so quietly that I had to strain to hear them. "I can't be with you and not want to touch you."

Fuck.

It wasn't fair to her, or to Cassius, for us to sneak around behind his back. "Do you still want to be with me?" I voiced the question in a low voice. I had to hear her say it, even though I was sure of the answer.

"Yes!" Her gaze flew back to mine. "I just think, for now, we should take a step back. You—we need to decide if this is all worth it."

I understood her subtext. She meant that *I* needed to decide if this was worth it. If she was worth it.

"Okay." Scrubbing my hand across my face, I breathed out heavily.

She gave me a sad smile and leaned forwards to press a soft kiss to my lips, before climbing off me. "I'm going back inside."

"Wait." I caught her hand as she turned to leave. "I want you to know that there's no one else. There won't be anyone else for me."

"Thank you." Her fingers lightly squeezed mine, and then she dropped my hand and disappeared back inside the house. I placed my head in my hands. How had this all gone so fucked up, so fast?

I wasn't left alone with my thoughts for long. "West!" There was the sound of pounding footsteps, and Lena appeared in the kitchen doorway, brandishing her phone. Excitement sparkled in her eyes, her sadness temporarily chased away. The change was so sudden, it took me aback, and I just stared at her, frowning. She continued. "Martin Smith. There's a dog fight. Tonight. Late. And we have the location."

I jumped into action. "Right. Tell Cade what's going on. He'll want to be in on this, and I trust him to come up with a plan. Text me the details when you have them, and I'll be there."

"Where are you going?" She stared at me as I swung off the seat and strode towards the door. Stopping in front of her, I leaned down to kiss her forehead softly before I drew back to meet her gaze.

"I'm going to get my best friend back."

The tracking app showed me Cassius' location, and when I turned into the car park, I saw his SUV in the far corner. Parking next to it, I checked my phone again. The tracking app wasn't so accurate that I could pinpoint exactly where he was, but it was accurate enough that it would give me his general vicinity. I headed down to the wooden pier that stretched out over the sea first, jogging down to the end, but he wasn't there. Stopping halfway back, I scanned the beach either side, but I couldn't see him.

I watched the gulls fighting over someone's discarded chips while I debated. A large black bird was perched on a rock below me, and as I watched, it hopped off the rock and disappeared under the pier.

Under the pier.

Without wasting any more time, I jogged back down the pier and onto the beach, making my way between the wooden struts that held the pier suspended above the ground.

"Cass."

He was sitting on a rock, throwing pebbles into the sea. When I spoke, he didn't acknowledge my presence. Yeah, he was definitely pissed off with me. I took a seat next to him. "Cass," I tried again.

Still no answer.

"Fucking talk to me, will you?"

At that, he finally turned to me, his eyes blazing. "What the fuck, West? Come to tell me more lies?"

"I wanted to give you time to cool off, but we don't have that time anymore. So just shut the fuck up and talk to me!"

"Which is it?" Some of the anger had left his tone.

"Which is what?"

"I can't shut the fuck up and talk to you, mate. Got to pick one or the other." Now there was a definite lift to the corner of his mouth.

"Mate? *Are* we still mates?" Picking up a pebble, I drew my arm back and threw it into the sea to give me something to do while I waited for his reply. Had I completely fucked things up between us?

He sighed. "Yeah."

That one word filled me with relief, and my shoulders dropped as I turned back to face him. "I wanna apologise. When I told you nothing was going on with Lena, I lied."

"No shit," he muttered, rolling his eyes.

"Yeah, well, I'm sorry, okay? If it helps, I've been really fucking stressed about the whole thing. I even went to my dad for advice."

He stared at me, surprised. "Seriously? Things must've been bad if you went to Arlo."

"His advice was sound, actually. He said I should talk to you."

"I always knew I liked him." Swiping another pebble from the ground, he threw it out to sea.

"Nice shot."

"I know."

Clearing my throat, I attempted to explain. "My head was messed up. Still is, to be honest. Me and Lena...we decided that we're not going to be together. So you don't need to worry about that."

"You're not together because of me?" His mouth twisted, like he wasn't sure how to feel about that.

"Not just that. It's just better that we take some time to think about what we want."

He nodded, his expression thoughtful. "Is she okay, though? Really okay? When she told me what had happened to her, it fucking killed me."

"Yeah, she's okay." Picking up a smooth grey stone from the ground, I turned it over in my palm. "She...I've been careful with her."

"If this is some reference to sex, don't tell me." Holding up his hand, he pulled a face. "I do *not* wanna hear anything about that, thanks."

"Noted."

"She's my sister. I'm just looking out for her."

"I know."

We fell into silence for a while then. When he eventually spoke, his voice was low. "I've never wanted to think about her with a boyfriend before." The face he pulled made me bite my lip, hard, to stop my laugh escaping. "And you. You're my wingman. What the fuck am I supposed to do now? No one to pick up women with."

"No more threesomes," I added helpfully.

"No more nights out."

"We're still doing that."

He smiled then, and it reached his eyes. "We'd better." Reaching down, he grabbed two stones, passing one to me, then throwing the other out to sea.

"Anyway, I'm not with Lena at the moment," I reminded him, before throwing the stone he'd given me. It hit one of the pier's wooden support posts.

"But if you could be, you would, right?" Cassius gave me a sidewards glance.

"Yeah," I admitted.

"Okay. Just promise me that you won't try to hide shit from me again. And don't hurt her, or I'll chop your fucking balls off."

"Leave my balls out of this." I cupped them protectively through my jeans, and he smirked, so I glared at him. "I don't think you have the balls to go near my balls."

He thought for a minute, then shrugged unconcernedly. "I'll ask Z to do it."

Before I could reply, my phone buzzed in my pocket. "It's Lena. We need to go." As we both climbed to our feet, I updated him on the Martin Smith situation, telling him everything I knew—which wasn't much. He frowned, picking his way over the stones back to the slope that led up to the paved area at the bottom of the pier. "This is another thing I'm really not happy about. She's so reckless sometimes."

"I know. I'll watch out for her. But you know how she can be."

Heading into the car park, I glanced down at his hand, holding his car keys. "How's your hand?"

"This hand?" He waved it in my face. "This hand that you made me punch a wall with?"

"Oh, we're blaming me, are we?"

"It seems fair."

"I guess."

"Thanks for your concern." His voice dripped with sarcasm. At my pointed look, he sighed. "It fucking hurts, actually."

"Sorry." I meant it.

"Nah, it's okay. Or it will be. Feels bruised." He pressed

the fingers of his other hand into his knuckles experimentally. "Yep, definitely bruised."

"You should've used your left hand."

"Yeah, because at the time, the first thought in my head was 'which hand would be better to slam into a wall?'"

"Try to remember for next time." I grinned at him.

"There better not be a next time," he warned me, his own grin stretching across his face. "I'm a lover, not a fighter."

"Yeah, alright." I rolled my eyes.

"It's true."

We reached our cars, and he stopped with his hand on the door. "Want to drop your car back at the house and take mine?"

"Yeah, okay." I went to get into my car but turned back to face him as he spoke my name.

"West?" His eyes met mine. "If I could pick anyone for Lena to be with, it would be you."

31

lena

We pulled up close to the location where the dog fight was supposedly taking place, parking in the shadows next to a red van with a huge dent in the side. No one had spoken much since we'd left the house, but Cassius and Weston had arrived back home at the same time, and West was sitting next to Cass in the passenger seat, so I was guessing they'd made up. One less thing to worry about. I wasn't exactly looking forward to having a conversation with my brother, but he deserved an apology from me, at least.

But now, we were here to investigate—to gather as much information as we could. My goal was simple—to break this dog-fighting ring. Weston's goal—to find something on Martin Smith.

Zayde's bike pulled up next to the SUV, and we reconvened outside. I tugged the wig over my ponytail and pulled up the hood of my hoodie.

"Are you wearing a wig?" Winter hissed, staring at me.

I grinned. "Yep. I thought maybe I should disguise myself."

"Ooh, good idea." She pushed my hood back, running her fingers over it. "Feels good. Looks good. Cade, do you think—"

"No." He tugged her into his arms, slamming his mouth over hers. Ugh. I heard him say something about how Winter's hair was too gorgeous to cover up, or something like that, and it honestly made me feel nauseous. I caught Weston's eye, and he had the same expression on his face.

"My brother is…" He trailed off with a shrug, still pulling a face.

"Yeah." I made a gagging motion before I sidled closer, dropping my voice. "How did it go with Cass?"

"Good, I think." He glanced over at my brother, who was showing Zayde something on his phone. "He threatened to have Z cut my balls off if I hurt you."

"Ha! I'd like to see him try." I smothered a laugh, and he pouted at me.

"You wanna see someone cut my balls off?"

"No. I'm kind of attached to your balls." A flash of heat went through me as a vivid image of me sucking his cock came to mind.

"Yeah, so am I. *Because they're attached to me!*" he hissed, and this time I had to bury my face in his shoulder to stifle my laughter.

"What's all this talk about balls?" Winter was suddenly in front of us, her eyebrow raised.

"Z wants to cut West's balls off," I informed her, and she spun on her heel.

"Zayde Lowry! I need to have a word with you." She marched over to him, and I watched as he stared at her blankly, then took a long, hard look at Weston.

Winter's voice drifted back towards us, saying something about a serial killer stare, and I glanced back at Weston, who wasn't even looking at Zayde.

He was looking at me.

My laughter died away as he reached out, gently tugging my hood back into place. "You're beautiful, whatever colour your hair is." A grin tugged at his lips as I stared at him mutely. "Just thought you should know."

Clearing his throat, he stepped back, his gaze flicking to Cassius', who watched us both silently. Why had everyone perfected these blank expressions? How was I supposed to know what they were thinking?

The moment was interrupted by Caiden beckoning us all closer. "Just like we discussed. This is recon only. Don't get caught, don't let yourself be recognised. If anyone does spot you..." His brows pulled together. "I guess you'll have to pretend that you're there to enjoy it. And on that note..."

He took a roll of money from his pocket, handing us each a small bundle. "This is just in case. Try to keep a low profile, but if anyone questions you, you can say you want to place a bet. I hope it won't have to come to that."

Shoving the money into my pocket, I glanced over at Winter. She was staring at the money in her hand uncertainly.

"Hey," I whispered to her. "You don't have to do this, you know. You can wait in the car."

"No! I'm not being left behind." Swallowing hard, she ran her thumb across the notes, before raising her gaze to mine. "I'm just not sure how I'm going to be able to act like I'm not bothered by what's happening in there. It affected me enough, just the glimpse I saw of it on the TV screens." Her hand fisted the money, crinkling it in her palm.

"Have you told Cade?"

"Yeah. He suggested I stay behind or out of the way." Her voice hardened. "Fuck. That."

"I'll tell you what. Come with me. I'm not planning on being detected by any of the fuckers here today. We're going to keep to the shadows and see if we can find out who's running this shitshow."

"Okay. Sounds good." Her voice lowered. "I kind of wanted to wear a wig."

"Next time, I'll get you one," I promised. She smiled at me and then turned to Caiden to tell him our plan. He nodded, relief clear in his eyes. Probably, if it was up to him, he'd keep her locked inside the car, away from any kind of harm.

We split, staying in pairs for safety, circling around to the waste ground where the fight was being held.

As we drew closer, I heard the noise. The whole area had been ringed by temporary fencing, tall metal sheets that were impossible to scale. From inside, there was the sound of shouts, talking, jeering, and the distinctive sound of snarling and whimpering. Winter sucked in a sharp breath, visibly steeling herself against the noise, before she squared her shoulders.

"These bastards are going down." Her tone was pure venom, and I shivered.

"Oh, yes, they are. Everyone here has blood on their hands. And we're going to make them pay." I held up my hand, and she slapped my palm, then gave me a savage grin.

"Let's bring them down."

We circled around the area and discovered that the fencing had another opening on one side. To the side of the opening was a small shipping container, and we darted into its shadows, crouching down, while we worked out a plan of action.

"Feel that?" I grabbed Winter's hand, pushing it against the cool metal. It vibrated under our palms.

"Is that…" She trailed off, pressing her ear to the container. "I can hear them." From inside the container came the noise of rattling cages and the sound of dogs in distress. "Fuck, this is horrible," she murmured. "Can we just sneak inside and set them free?"

"No." I sighed. "These dogs…they're not like normal dogs. They've been bred for one purpose only—to fight. That's all they know; all they've been taught."

"What does that mean for these dogs?" she whispered, her face falling.

"It means that sometimes the kindest thing to do is to have them put down."

"That's so sad." Tears filled her eyes. "They can't be rehabilitated or retrained or something?"

"Sometimes they can. Some are lucky. But not always."

"We need to stop these people from doing this." Her voice was resolute.

"We will. Let me think for a minute." My eyes swept the area. A bell sounded, and the shouts increased in volume. "Okay, now. While the fight is just beginning." We crept towards the fence opening, staying in the shadows. There was a huge, beefy guy standing next to the entrance, bulging arms folded across his chest.

"How are we gonna get past him?"

"First option, we wait until he's distracted, then sneak inside. Second option, one of us distracts him while the other sneaks inside."

"I don't like the second option." Winter shook her head at me. "We stick together."

"Okay. Come on." Reaching out, I grabbed her hand. "When I say, we go. I'll watch the guy; you keep an eye out for anyone else."

She gave me a brief nod, already focused on our surroundings. I kept my eyes on the guard, watching as he pulled a crumpled pack of cigarettes from his pocket and fished one out. With agonising slowness, he lifted it to his lips. The strong breeze whipped the flame of his lighter, and he turned towards the fence, cupping his hand over it to shield it from the wind.

"Now!" We darted inside the enclosure, keeping low to the ground and hugging the fence.

Inside was chaos.

We'd entered from the same point that the dogs came from. There was a large circular pit, hollowed out of the ground, surrounded by low chain-link fencing with an opening on one side. The whole thing was lit by some kind of portable floodlights, throwing us into shadow.

A crowd ringed the pit, maybe around sixty or so. Not a huge number by any means, but any number of people was bad in my opinion. The fact that anyone would want to be entertained by something like this. It sickened me.

At the far end of the pit, a guy in black combats and a black shirt held up a small camera, focused on the ring, and I carefully tugged Winter close so that I could speak right in her ear. "Camera."

She squeezed my hand, letting me know she'd seen it, before melting further into the shadows.

Everyone was intently focused on the two dogs in the pit, snapping and snarling at one another. Taking out my phone, I began to record.

Within a couple of minutes, the fight was over. I had to turn away as the twitching, bloody body was dragged out of the pit, while the victor was held in place by a metal collar attached to a pole held by one of the men, that seemed to tighten and choke the dog every time it tried to lunge forwards.

"What do you say, gentlemen?" A loud voice suddenly boomed around us, rebounding off the fencing. "Shall we make this final fight a little more interesting?" Heads turned towards a guy with a microphone, standing on something that made him tower above everything else. A huge hood obscured most of his face.

"Because of course he had to wear the biggest hood known to man. Couldn't make it easy for us," I muttered under my breath.

"Place your bets! This time, the fight will be a three-way death match!" The pure pleasure in his voice chilled me to my core.

The screen that was rigged up behind him on some kind of crane-type thing lit up with images and stats for each of the three dogs. Money began to exchange hands, the volume of the crowd increasing again. Most of the time, the fights ended without death (or at least, in the ring), but the death matches seemed to be a particular favourite of these spectators. The organisers would use dogs that had outlived their usefulness for one reason or another and put them in a fight, literally to the death.

Three separate cages were dragged into the enclosure, and the men worked with practised precision, positioning them ready to enter the ring. They held what looked like cattle prods, and when one of the men jabbed it into the side of the cage, it took everything I had in me to not rush over to him and jab that prod into his belly.

"I want to shove that prod right into his balls," Winter all but growled, staring daggers at him.

"I was thinking his stomach."

"Either works." She shrugged. "He needs a taste of how it feels. Those poor dogs."

The crowd quietened when microphone man called for silence, waiting with bated breath as the first two cages were opened and the dogs were herded into the ring, complete with the same kind of collar as the dogs in the previous fight. They lunged at each other, but the men holding them kept them apart as the third dog was pushed into the pit. I kept my camera recording, panning around the area so I could take in as many details as possible, then analyse it later.

Next to me, Winter trembled. "I hate this so much," she whispered, forcing her eyes onto the crowds, away from the sight of the animals in the pit.

My spine prickled.

Then, the whistle blew.

A large hand clamped over my mouth.

And chaos reigned again.

32

weston

"Evening." Cassius strode up to the guy at the entrance without a care in the world, all confident, careless swagger. Falling in line with him, I let him do the talking.

"Fifty pounds entry fee," the guy said in a bored voice, holding out his hand. Cassius peeled off a few of the notes Caiden had given him, and the guy shone his torch over them before nodding and stepping aside. "Have a good evening, gentlemen."

Then, we were inside.

Cassius spoke out of the side of his mouth, keeping his voice low. "Cade and Z can do the sneaky shit. We'll hide in plain sight. Keep your hood up. Both of us could be recognised if any of the Alstone lot are here. If anyone does recognise us, we know what to do."

I gave him a brief nod. We melted into the crowd, outwardly casual, but I knew both of us were on high alert. Cass indicated to a free space close to the fence, and we made our way through the press of bodies.

The whistle sounded to mark the beginning of the fight.

Instead of focusing on the two dogs, I scanned the faces of the people across from me. Almost all were men, some in suits despite our shady wasteland location, and others dressed more casually, as I was, in jeans and hoodies. Tugging my hood further over my head, I stared, unseeing, down into the pit, perfecting the look I used to give my English teacher when he started quoting Shakespeare at the class. Seeing, but unseeing, my head a million miles away.

"This is kind of sickening." Cassius' voice was so quiet that I would've missed it, if he hadn't pressed his mouth right up to my ear, all wet and warm.

"You know what's sickening?" I returned the favour, turning my head to him. "You practically kissing my ear."

"You fucking wish." And just because he was Cassius, he stuck his tongue out and licked my earlobe.

"Mate! What the fuck?" I spun around to stare at him. "Seriously?"

His shoulders shook as he tried to suppress his laughter. "You should see your face right now."

"Cass," I warned, my voice low, and he glanced up, realising we'd attracted the attention of at least two other guys in our immediate vicinity.

His gaze snapped to the dogs, his humour immediately dying away. "Bite the bastard," he muttered, loud enough for the guy next to him to hear and voice his approval for that statement. I breathed out in relief—his questionable sense of humour wouldn't go unnoticed here. We watched in silence for a while, or gave the impression of watching, at least. The fight was over quickly, though, so we had a reprieve.

"Who the fuck is that?" We both turned to stare at the

man who'd climbed on top of a podium to address the crowd.

Not really a podium, but a large metal crate. Whatever, it put him on a level above the rest of us. Dressed in a black-on-black suit, with a long black hooded coat that almost looked like a cloak, he appeared intimidating and almost inhuman. The hood obscured most of his face, but when he turned slightly, I caught a glimpse of grey swept-back hair underneath.

Martin Smith.

Yes.

Digging my phone from my pocket, I shielded it between my palms and hit the camera button, pointing it directly at him. Would this be enough evidence for my dad? Probably not, but I continued to take photos before I switched to the video function.

I nudged Cassius to draw his attention to where Martin Smith was standing, and he gave a subtle indication of his head to let me know he'd seen him, too.

Another hooded guy across the pit caught my eye, weaving in and out of the crowds with practised ease, and I watched money exchanging hands from the people crowding around the pit barrier.

From his position on the podium, Smith tilted his head in the direction of the guy and received a subtle nod in response.

Who were they to each other?

Was this the Thom that had been mentioned in the message from Martin Smith's phone?

I had no answers, and for now, all I could do was bide my time and hope that we stumbled across something useful.

"West!" Cassius spoke urgently in my ear, and now

there was no humour in his voice. My eyes flew to his, and he mouthed the words, *We need to leave, now*.

Nodding, I stepped backwards, glad that the spectators behind me were more interested in getting a good view than why I was moving in the opposite direction to the fight. Cassius followed in my wake, affecting his casual, confident persona, and I attempted to do the same even though my heart was in my fucking throat. I didn't even know what he'd seen, all I knew was the urgency in his tone that meant we had to get out of there right now.

We broke out of the crowd, and I paused for a second to get my bearings. Cassius didn't let me stop, gripping my elbow and moving in the direction of the exit.

The security guy barely spared us a glance, too busy looking at his phone. To be fair, he was probably more interested in who was coming in than who was going out.

When we were a safe distance away, Cassius flopped against the red brick wall of the building next to us. "Fuck me, that was close."

"Why did we suddenly need to leave?" I didn't get it.

"I saw Z's dad," he explained. "There was no way... We could have lied our way through most situations, but he would've seen straight through us."

"I didn't even see him."

He grinned, patting my shoulder. "That's what you have me for. We're a team. I watched out for shit like that, while you kept an eye on Martin Smith, right?"

"Yeah." I nodded slowly. When he put it that way, it didn't seem so bad. Maybe my video would help us. Whatever, we already knew he was involved, and now we had solid video evidence.

We made our way back to Cass' SUV and waited for the others inside, reclining our seats and talking about nothing and everything. I was relieved that my best mate wasn't someone to hold a grudge, and he was acting like he normally would with me.

The time stretched.

"Where are the others?" My heart rate picked up. Surely they should've been back by now.

He glanced at the clock on his dashboard. "Good question. We should probably..." His words trailed off as his eyes went to something in front of us, and I followed his gaze to see the others running in our direction.

"Go! Go!" Winter collapsed breathlessly into the back seat, closely followed by Lena, and Cassius wasted no time in starting up the engine. As he spun the car away from the kerb, I saw Zayde's bike shoot past us, Caiden on the back.

"What happened?" Twisting in my seat, I stared at the girls.

"We'll tell you when we get home" was all Winter said, and I had to be satisfied with that. Turning up the music on the radio because it was clear that no one felt like talking, I settled back in my seat and stared out at the road with unseeing eyes.

We were all together and accounted for. We had video footage. I just hoped that we could work this shit out and put it all behind us.

33

lena

The house was quiet, sombre almost. We'd assembled in the kitchen, seated around the dining table. Weston was next to me, his hand finding mine under the table.

He'd dragged me aside the second we'd got home.

"Are you okay?" He gripped my chin in his hands, staring down at me with a look of concern.

I blew out a shaky breath. "Yeah, I'm okay. I promise."

He studied me intently, his other hand sliding around my back and pulling me closer to him. I felt the heat of his body against mine, and I reached up to thread my arms around his neck.

"I'm fine," I repeated. "How are you?"

His eyes widened.

"What, you didn't think I wouldn't worry about you?" I whispered the words against his lips.

He shook his head slowly. "I thought...I guess I thought you'd be focused on your own thing."

"Never." With effort, I untangled myself from him. "This isn't us keeping our distance, is it? We're doomed."

A small smile crossed his face. "It's just two friends showing concern for each other."

"Yeah, buddy." I punched his arm playfully.

"Do me a favour? Never call me 'buddy' again."

"You don't like it?" I teased, grinning at him.

He didn't reply but instead leaned back against the wall, keeping his distance this time. "Are you sure you're okay?"

"Yeah, I really am."

"Good."

Now, he squeezed my hand before letting me go, his fingers releasing me one by one, as if he didn't want to relinquish his grip on me.

"Okay. Who wants to go first?" Caiden spoke up, looking around at us all.

"I will." Cassius detailed his and West's experience, including the fact that the figure on the podium was Martin Smith, something we hadn't been able to tell from our position. As he spoke, he kept glancing over at Zayde.

"What is it?" Zayde eventually asked.

"Uh...I saw your dad there. Sorry, mate."

Zayde looked down at the table, saying nothing, and Cassius rushed to fill the sudden silence. "I panicked, had to get us out of there before he saw us. There was no way we would have been able to stay under the radar with him there."

"I think we got what we came for anyway. Plenty of video footage." Weston tapped his phone. "I haven't had time to go through it yet, but I'm sure it'll throw up some interesting shit."

"So there was another guy going around collecting bets? Any ideas who that was?" I asked the table in general.

"No fucking clue," Caiden said. "I didn't get a good look at him, either." He glanced over at Zayde, who shrugged.

"I was too busy fending off Lena's attack."

That made me laugh. "Sorry, but if someone comes up behind me and slams their hand over my mouth, what am I supposed to do? Just sit there and let it happen? You could've been anyone."

"No. You did good. You've got decent moves."

From my side, Weston gave a low growl at Zayde's words of praise, and my eyes flew to his in time to catch his frown. Guess this new possessive streak was as much a surprise to him as it was to me.

I noticed Cassius watching us both from across the table, so I shuffled a bit further away from Weston. Just to make it clear that we were taking the whole just being friends thing seriously. He raised a brow, then smirked at me. *I hate you*, I mouthed, and a laugh burst from his lips.

"Something funny?"

Cassius turned to Caiden. "Nope."

"Okay, if you're finished, I'll go through what I discovered with Zayde." Caiden detailed how he and Zayde had circled the wider area around the waste ground, documenting car number plates as they searched for the vehicle that had transported the dogs. "We hit the jackpot. There was a lorry parked under the motorway bridge. Totally nondescript, just a usual haulier's truck, but the fact that there were no distinctive markings made me stop. Then I noticed the Romanian plates, and I remembered that you said the latest batch of dogs had been transported from Romania."

"The lock was laughably easy to open." Zayde took over,

his disdainful look showing just what he thought of the truck's security. "Inside..."

Caiden held up his phone, turning it so we could all see. "I'll get these up on the TV screen later, but you can see behind all these boxes are the cages, and those sacks in the corner are dog food. The whole of the inside fucking stank of dogs." He continued by telling us how he and Zayde had left the truck and circled back around to the waste ground. It had been pure luck that they'd come in at the side we were on. The security guy had spotted us—or so the boys had deduced by the way he'd started in our direction, so they'd incapacitated him, then got us out of there as quickly as they could.

Winter went through our experience, and I forwarded my video footage to West, before uploading it to our secure storage. Then I wiped every trace of it from my phone.

You could never be too careful. Promethium had recently told us the story of one of his agents who had incriminating video evidence on his phone. The agent had been investigating a gang in East London who were rumoured to have been involved in sex trafficking. He hadn't been caught at the time of obtaining the video footage, but around a week later, one of the gang members caught up with him. They'd had their suspicions about him, and when the gang member had taken his phone, the video footage that was still stored on there was enough to incriminate him.

They'd recovered his body from the river a few days later.

Of course, it could have been a cautionary tale made up by Promethium to make sure that we stayed safe, but either way, it was a risk to keep that kind of stuff on our phones.

Thankfully our Kryptos app was secure enough that it

would take an expert hacker to crack. Not only that, it was disguised as an everyday phone app, so it would appear innocent unless you were already aware of it.

"I'm gonna go through all this shit and see what I can come up with," Weston announced, standing up and stretching. My gaze was drawn to the ridges of his abs as his T-shirt rode up, and heat flashed in his eyes as he looked down to catch me staring at him.

Like I'd told him earlier, we were doomed.

I'd had a taste of him, and I wanted more.

One thing that had been drilled into me by every single one of my various martial arts instructors, though, was discipline.

I had the discipline to resist Weston until we'd had time to process whatever this was between us. Until he was sure of what he wanted.

But when his eyes met mine again, I wasn't sure I wanted to resist anymore.

34

lena

After a night in the guest room, I was woken by a call from my mum.

"Are we ever going to see you?" were her first words when I answered.

"Sorry, Mum. I'm at Cassius' place. I did text you to say."

She hummed noncommittally. "Is Weston there?"

"Um. He's not in the room with me. He's somewhere in the house, I guess."

"I want you to invite him for Sunday lunch." She adopted a stern tone, making me roll my eyes.

"Why would I invite him? Cassius should do it, he's his best friend."

"No. I want you to do it." Her voice lowered. "It's for Cassius' birthday. We know he'll be busy celebrating with his friends, but your dad and I wanted to do a family thing."

I sighed. "Fine. Am I inviting anyone else to this thing, or what?"

"Invite whoever you see fit. I want to keep it small, a

family feel, so maybe just invite the rest of the group and a few others?"

"Okay." I already knew that this was going to be the opposite of a "small" thing, but there was no point mentioning that to my mum. She loved to entertain. To be fair, Cass loved a party, even more so if he was the centre of attention, so I knew he'd be happy.

We chatted for a few more minutes before she ended the call, and then I made my way downstairs to see who else was around. Cassius was in the kitchen, setting out breakfast supplies, while Winter was pouring boiling water from the kettle into a series of mugs grouped on the countertop.

"Ugh, Cass. Do you have to parade around in just your boxers?"

Winter turned to face me, kettle in hand. "You know he cooks naked sometimes?"

"Gross. Please put some clothes on." I grabbed an apron from the hook on the back of the door and threw it at him.

"Ah. My favourite apron. Thanks, sis." He smirked at me, pulling it over his head and adjusting it so the words "Warning: Concealed Sausage" were in full view.

"I just can't with you," I muttered, turning away and crossing over to Winter. With a subtle combination of me typing out a message for her to read and several pointed looks, I'd invited her to the Sunday lunch. She said she'd take care of inviting Caiden and Zayde, so I guessed it was up to me to deal with West.

Not that I minded.

"How long will breakfast be?" I asked my brother.

He replied with his head buried in the fridge, pulling out ingredients. "About twenty minutes. You want your eggs scrambled?"

"Fried, please." I backed away towards the door.

"It's scrambled or nothing," he informed me.

"I guess I'll have them scrambled, then." Before I left the kitchen, I added, "Thanks," because regardless of his egg cooking preferences, it was nice of him to cook for me without me asking.

The doorbell sounded, and since I was in the hallway, I padded over to the front door. Kinslee, Winter's close friend, stood on the other side, and she gave me a bright smile when she saw me.

"Morning! I wasn't expecting to see you here. Is Winter around?"

"Kitchen." I stepped aside to let her in. "Morning, by the way." Because I knew she'd slept with Weston and I clearly had issues, I didn't return her smile.

Her brows pulled together, and she eyed me uncertainly.

"Okay. Thanks," she eventually said and disappeared off down the hallway. I suddenly had a need to find Weston and remind him that even though we were currently not together, there was no other girl for him. No one except me.

The door to the computer room was ajar, and I could see the back of his head through the crack, his dark hair all tousled. Slipping unnoticed into the room because he was engrossed in his computer, I came up behind him and put a hand on the back of his chair. "Hi." I spun his chair so he was facing me and straddled his thighs.

"Hi." The frown he'd been wearing just seconds ago melted away, replaced with a huge grin. "What's all this for?"

I wound my arms around his neck and placed a kiss to his cheek, feeling the scratchiness of his light stubble against my lips. "Just wanted to say good morning to my friend."

"Friends kiss each other, right?" His grin widened. "On the lips?"

"Yeah. I'm sure that's a thing."

He slid his hand up to my back and pressed a soft kiss on my mouth.

"That kiss didn't seem friendly enough to me." I attempted a thoughtful face. "Should we try again?"

He nodded. "Yeah. I think we need to perfect it."

He kissed me again.

And again.

And again.

Until I was breathless, clinging onto him, melting against his body.

"Mmmm. Good morning," he murmured, his voice a sexy rasp as he finally drew back. "I think we perfected the friends kiss."

"Yep." I tried to sound casual, but my voice was so breathy that there was no disguising the effect he had on me. In an effort to rein things in, I turned the subject to Cassius' surprise lunch.

"I'll be there," he promised me, then spun the chair back around. Lifting me effortlessly, he turned me around to face the computer. "Look at this." He leaned forwards, clicking the computer mouse. "Recognise the names on this list?"

I ran my gaze down the list of names, recognising some of them. "What's this? Is this a list of the people that were there yesterday?"

"Yeah." His hand moved from where it had been resting against my side, and I twisted around to look at him. He was rubbing his brow, his eyes closed.

"West?" My hand covered his. He sighed, his breath skating across my cheek.

"Just a headache."

Pulling his hand away, I stroked my fingers across his brow and across to his temples. He groaned, keeping his eyes closed, his lashes fanned out across his cheeks.

Fuck. He was beautiful.

With an effort, I focused on the reason I had my hands on him to begin with. "West?"

"Yeah?" He kept his eyes closed, his arms lightly gripping my sides, his head resting against the back of his chair.

"How long have you had these headaches?"

His eyes blinked open, glassy and unfocused as I continued the movements of my fingers. "I dunno. A while."

"When you're looking at the screen, or other times?" I slid my hands into his hair, massaging his head, and he groaned, his eyes falling shut again.

"Fuck. Keep doing that."

"When?"

He was silent for a bit, contemplating my question. "When I look at the screen."

Gripping his face, I examined him. "Open your eyes."

After a couple of minutes, he opened them, watching me. The deep, dark blues and greens and greys were so hypnotic, I almost lost my train of thought.

"Have you had an eye test?"

"I don't need glasses," he said automatically.

"Will you just have one? For me?" I attempted to bat my eyelashes and pout.

His laughter was so loud, I was surprised that no one else came running to see what was so funny. "Don't do that again," he wheezed. If I didn't like him so much, I would have been tempted to cause him physical pain.

Actually, I was still tempted.

"Sorry," he muttered, when he finally had control of himself. "Promise me you won't do that again."

"Do. What," I bit out.

His hands cupped my face. "Believe me when I say that you're beautiful, Lena." He stared into my eyes, sincerity radiating from him, although his lips were still curved in amusement. "You don't need any tricks to get me to do what you want." He buried his face in my shoulder, his arms wrapping tightly around me.

"Okay," I agreed readily. "But will you have an eye test? Please?"

"Yeah. I'll book one." His voice came out muffled but resigned, before he raised his head. "I will. Promise."

"Good." I didn't linger on the conversation because it was clear he didn't want to talk about it. Instead, I returned the attention to the list of names as I turned back to face the screen. "Do you—"

Before I could even finish the sentence, he was scrolling to the bottom of the list. "These are the people who I think could be running it."

He dragged the cursor across the screen, highlighting the few names listed in bold.

Martin Smith
Jaroslaw Milosz
Thom ???

"Okay, let's go through these. We have Martin Smith. Do we know his role?"

His thumb stroked across my stomach almost absentmindedly, like he didn't realise he was doing it. "I'm sure he's the money man. Sorting out the deals, or whatever.

"I think so, too." Everything I knew ran through my mind as I tried to fit the puzzle pieces into place. "What about this Jaroslaw guy?"

He leaned forwards again, navigating to another folder where he opened a file labelled Milosz. "This is what I have on him." Scrolling through the data he had, I learned that Jaroslaw had a criminal record in Poland, and he had been tentatively connected with a trafficking ring in Romania. But the one thing that made his connection crystal clear? He was the licensed owner of the lorry that Caiden and Zayde had found.

"Do you think he's the one bringing the dogs in?"

West shrugged. "It seems like it."

"What about Thom?" My eyes focused on that one word, typed in bold with a load of question marks next to it.

"I don't know." He heaved a sigh, dragging me back against him at the same time. "He was mentioned in that message from Martin Smith's phone, wasn't he?"

I nodded, thinking back to the messages and what we knew of the guys already.

"Do you think he could be the guy in the hood that was collecting the bets at the fight?" I wondered aloud.

"Could be. That was my first thought, but fuck knows. There are a lot of people involved in this shit."

"That's true." We both stared at the screen, Weston's head leaning on my shoulder while he navigated through the data.

"See that?" He opened up a record of import. "Fits with the date that was mentioned in that email, remember?"

"This looks cosy."

An overly loud voice sounded from behind us, and I felt

rather than heard Weston's sigh in my ear. He spun us around lazily, until we were both facing my brother.

The expression on Cassius' face...I couldn't read it. It was like he was happy, and not happy at the same time. Like he didn't know whether to be pleased with us or not.

"You wanna see my list?" Weston offered, and Cassius blinked, then nodded.

"Yeah, mate. Show me what you got."

"Is breakfast ready?" My stomach suddenly decided to make itself known.

"Almost. I left Z in charge." Cassius flashed me a smile, and I climbed off Weston, needing to leave them alone.

"I'm gonna keep an eye on him." I escaped the room and made my way to the kitchen, where Caiden and Zayde were finishing up the food prep while Winter and Kinslee set everything out on the table.

"What can I do to help?"

It was Caiden who answered me. "Get the salt and pepper."

After I did that, I slid into a seat on the left side of the table. "Breakfast is a big deal here, huh?" I stared at the spread laid out in front of me.

"Yep." My brother had re-entered the room with Weston, and he took over from Zayde, dishing out the eggs onto everyone's plates. "Take a seat."

"I already did."

He rolled his eyes in response, concentrating on dishing out the food. My attention focused on Kinslee. She barely paid attention to West, and I relaxed against my chair.

"What do you think, Kins?" Cassius spoke, turning my attention back to her unwillingly. She shrugged, her eyes dancing, amused by whatever my brother had said when I wasn't paying attention.

"I have no idea," she drawled. "I'll let you decide."

Because I was clearly a masochist, I slid out of my chair and spoke in Kinslee's ear. "Do you want to come to Cassius' birthday lunch?"

Her eyes met mine, all wide, amber pools, fringed by heavy black lashes. Why did she have to be so fucking pretty? And why the fuck did I even care? This stupid, irrational jealousy over Weston needed to go away. Now. "I'd like that." Her eyes narrowed. "If you're okay with it."

Apparently, I was way too easy to read.

"I'm fine with that."

She gave me a knowing look. "Lena."

"What."

Her voice lowered so it was barely above a whisper. She scooped food onto her fork with one hand, while still focusing on me.

"Weston never looked at me the way he looks at you."

I didn't know I needed to hear those words until she said them.

Something inside me settled, and I smiled at her for real.

35

lena

After breakfast, Winter decided that she wanted to hang out with me and Kinslee while the boys played football. It was raining hard outside, so our options were limited.

"What about Skirmish?" I named the huge warehouse-style place owned by Credence Pope, aka Creed, that offered everything from archery to paintballing.

"Let's do it. I wanna improve my knife-throwing skills."

Winter's enthusiasm caught me off guard, and I looked to Kinslee, who shrugged. "I'm good with that, if you can book us a slot with short notice."

After a quick call to the centre, we booked one of the throwing ranges, which allowed up to eight people at once.

"Should we invite someone else? Make it an even number?" Winter suggested to me. "Why don't you invite one of your friends from Alstone High? It's time I got to know them, really. Especially since I have a feeling that you're going to be spending a lot more time around here."

"What's that supposed to mean?"

"West." She coughed into her hand, and I rolled my eyes as Kinslee laughed.

"So subtle."

One more phone call later, and we were on our way to Skirmish, stopping to pick up Raine on the way. After her initial shyness, Raine was coaxed into a conversation with us about her clothing designs. I happened to mention the leggings she'd designed for me, and by the time we'd pulled into the Skirmish car park, she'd agreed to design a pair for both Winter and Kinslee.

Inside, we were shown to the throwing range and took up position. The others made me go first, supposedly so I could give the rest of them tips. Raine wasn't bad, for a beginner, and soon we were all involved in the game, trying to be the first to hit the centre.

While Raine and Kinslee took their turns, Winter sidled up to me. "I've been meaning to speak to you. What's going on now with you and West?"

I sank to the floor of the range, leaning my head back against the wall, and she took a seat next to me. Stretching my legs out in front of me, I thought for a minute. "We both agreed to take a step back. Mostly to give Cass a chance to cool off, and..." My voice lowered. "I wanted him to make sure that this was what he wanted. If this was worth it. If *I* was worth it, you know?"

She shuffled closer, leaning her head on my shoulder. "West would be lucky to have you. I agree that he should be sure of what he wants, but if you want my opinion—and too bad if you don't, because you're getting it anyway—he's really into you. Really, really into you. If he hasn't already come to that conclusion by himself, I'm sure it won't take him long to realise."

I tilted my head to rest on top of hers. "Thanks. I hope so. I've liked him for so long."

"I know, I could always tell," she said with a small laugh. "I don't think it was obvious to anyone else, though."

"I hope not." I cringed.

We sat in silence for a few minutes, watching Kinslee and Raine. "You know what, though? We both have amazing taste in men. The Cavendish brothers are fucking hot." She lifted her head to grin at me.

"I think they're the ones with amazing taste." Climbing to my feet, I offered her my hand, pulling her up from the floor.

"That's true." We made our way back over to Kinslee and Raine, where she handed me a knife. "Are you going to stop holding back now and show us how it's done?"

"If you insist."

After our allotted time on the throwing range was up, we headed into the attached café area to get drinks. Queuing to pay, we were informed that our drinks were complimentary. Winter was just about to question it, when a smooth, male voice came from behind us.

"Afternoon, ladies."

I turned to see Creed, owner of Skirmish, his lips curving into a smile as he took the four of us in. His large muscular body was covered in grey suit trousers and a white shirt, and he had a suit jacket draped casually over one arm. His golden eyes glimmered with humour as Kinslee visibly flinched, and I bit my lip, trying not to laugh as I remembered the first time she'd been introduced to him. She'd had the same reaction then, too.

"Creed. I'm guessing you're the one behind our free drinks?" Winter smiled at him. He inclined his head.

"I am. I was making the rounds, stopping in on my way

back to London, when I noticed your car outside," he told her. "Couldn't leave without saying hi."

"This is Raine," I interjected, giving my friend a gentle nudge forwards. Unsurprisingly, she had a similar reaction to Kinslee, which seemed to amuse Creed even more.

"Always a pleasure." He stepped away from us, lifting his hand. "Drinks, food—whatever you want, it's on Skirmish."

After he'd gone, we made our way to a large table in the corner of the café. "That guy gives off some seriously scary vibes, doesn't he?" Raine pulled the wrapper off her straw. "Or was it just me?"

"Thank you!" Kinslee exclaimed. "I'm glad I'm not the only one who thinks so."

Winter laughed, leaning back in her chair. "He's gorgeous, though, isn't he?"

"Yes," we all agreed at once, then laughed.

"He's a good guy," she continued. "Or maybe good isn't the right word, because he's neither good or bad. He's...he's just...Creed."

"Yeah, that guy is all kinds of shades of grey." I dug in my pocket for my phone, which was buzzing annoyingly.

"Fifty shades?"

"Ha ha. I heard there were like a hundred different actual shades."

I tuned out the conversation as I saw the name on my screen and navigated straight to my messages.

West: Having fun?
Me: Yeah. I got the highest score in knife throwing *grin emoji*
West: No surprise. You've got skills

A smile spread across my face.

Me: What are you doing?

A few minutes passed before I got the next message, and it was worth the short wait. He'd sent me a selfie of himself, Cass, Cade, and Z, all hot and sweaty from their football match. He was grinning straight at the camera, at me, while Caiden had my brother in a headlock and Zayde was tipping water over his own head. He'd written "just finished football" under the picture.

My smile grew wider, and when I received the next message, I knew I was grinning like a lunatic.

West: Wish you were here

I set the image as my phone wallpaper, then sent back a one-word reply.

Me: Same

Under a minute later, another message came through.

West: Do you need a lift home? I feel like taking my baby for a drive now it's not raining
Me: I'm assuming you're referring to your car as your baby AGAIN *eyeroll emoji* But if you want a drive I won't say no
West: 20 mins. Wait for me

36

weston

My DBS rolled to a stop outside Skirmish, and my gaze went straight to Lena, waiting outside the entrance. When she saw me, a smile curved over her lips, and my heart stuttered. Her smile grew wider when she slid into the car, and I loved that I was the one to put a smile on her face.

"Hi." Leaning across the car, I cupped my hand around the back of her neck and drew her into a kiss. She pulled away much too quickly for my liking, laughing at whatever face I was pulling.

"Hi, *friend*." She emphasised the word, making me groan.

"Don't remind me."

Another laugh escaped her. Clipping her seat belt into place, she turned her attention to the view as I navigated away from Skirmish. "Where are we going?"

"Dunno." Pausing at the car park exit, I glanced in both directions before manoeuvring onto the road. "I just felt like driving, and I wanted to see you."

"Oh." Her voice was quiet, almost unsure. I felt her eyes

on me as I turned the wheel to the right, heading back in the direction of Alstone. Fuck, I wanted to touch her so badly.

"Talk to me," I said instead.

We talked for over an hour about anything and everything as I drove around without a destination in mind. Even though we'd known each other all our lives, everything felt new. Which I guess it was—we were connecting on a different level now.

After a while, the sidewards glances began again. From both of us. When we stopped at a set of traffic lights, my hand "accidentally" brushed over her thigh. As we sat in another queue of traffic, she repaid the favour, stroking dangerously close to my swelling dick with a sultry as fuck smile on her lips.

I couldn't take much more of this.

Once we hit the coastal road, I drove for a while longer before bringing the car to a stop on the clifftops. Next to us, a winding path led down to a small cove, but it was raining again, so I remained in my seat, reclining it back as far as it would go and unclipping my seat belt.

My eyes met Lena's.

The atmosphere in the car thickened.

In a flash, she was out of her seat and straddling me.

"I want you so fucking much." My voice was hoarse against her ear.

I half expected her to remind me of the friends thing again, but all she said was "There's not much room."

"Mmm. We can make it work." Kissing down her neck, I slid my hands under her top, stroking across her skin. "Tell me what you want."

"You. I want you." She ground herself down on my dick. Fuck. I needed her.

Even though I didn't want to stop, I had to make sure. Raising my head, I stared into her darkened eyes. "Even though we're—"

"Friends with benefits," she murmured against my lips, and I smiled. Yeah, I was in total agreement with her.

I carefully turned her around on top of me, helping her to slide her leggings down her legs. She kicked them off along with her boots, then pressed back against me, tilting her head and baring her neck to me.

"Mmm." I took the hint, dropping kisses down her throat as my finger skimmed over her underwear. She was so fucking ready for me. "You want this just as much as me, don't you?"

"Yes," she moaned, her hand pressing over mine, stilling my fingers. "Please."

Turning her back around, I took a minute to take in the sight of her panting and ready for me. There was something so fucking hot about her being mostly dressed, both of us out in the open, even though the rain was coming down and we were in a remote area. She made a small whimpering sound, and my cock jumped. Fuck, I needed to be inside her.

I unbuttoned my jeans, raising my hips to pull them down.

"Let me." She freed my cock, palming it, driving me insane with her touch. I shoved aside her underwear, and she lowered herself onto me, sliding down my thick length.

"You feel so tight around me. So fucking good." I groaned. "Touch yourself while I fuck you."

She nodded mutely as I began to move. My seat was as far back as it would go, but there was still hardly any space. When she looked at me like that, though, I knew it wouldn't be long before she was coming all over my cock.

We moved together, her hand slipping down between us to touch herself as I thrust up into her.

So fucking sexy.

The windows of my DBS steamed up as our movements became more urgent. "I'm gonna come," I rasped against her throat. "Tell me you're close." I ran my hands over her ass, pulling her even closer, our breathing coming in pants.

"*Yes*." She moaned the word as she buried her face in my neck, working her fingers over her clit as my hands gripped her ass, moving her against me. "Oh, fuuuuckk." She shuddered around me, crying out my name as she came, and it wasn't long before I was following her over the edge, arching back as my cock pulsed inside her.

We held on to each other, recovering, and she eventually straightened up—as much as she could in the limited space we had.

"So fucking good." I kissed her softly. "You okay?"

"Never better." Her eyes were shining, and a huge smile stretched across her lips. "I thought I might whack my head on the roof of the car, but it would've been worth it."

"I'm impressed we managed without injury," I told her, reaching out and smoothing her hair back down.

With another smile, she climbed off me carefully and fell back into her own seat, pulling her leggings and boots back on. Stretching out my cramped muscles, I grinned. Yeah, that had been worth every second of the discomfort of our confined positions.

"You're not in any rush to get back, are you?" She reclined back in her seat. "I'm kind of relaxed here."

"Nope. I'm not in any rush. I like being here with you." I flipped the radio back on, letting it play softly in the background. "You wanna talk more?"

"Yeah."

"Good." Reaching across the centre of the car, I found her hand and slid her fingers between mine. "Tell me how you got to be Mercury."

A soft laugh escaped her. "Okay. One evening when I couldn't sleep, I thought I might as well try out this new script I'd written, to see if it would get me into this system…"

As she began to tell her story, I closed my eyes, just listening to her speak.

There was nowhere else I'd rather be.

37

weston

N ow we had the list of names, we had somewhere to start, and I spent the week systematically going through it, while I continued to sift through the information coming in from Martin's texts and emails and Lena monitored his calls. As far as we could figure, most of the names were those whose only involvement was to attend or bet on the fights. I'd added another two names to my original list of three, and from what I could work out, they were involved in setting up the fights —equipment, locations, and so on.

"Focus on chapter twelve, and I'll expect your completed essays back on Monday."

I stared up from my laptop to see my marketing professor addressing the packed lecture theatre. Fuck, I hadn't been paying attention—too concerned with the whole Martin Smith situation. "What did he say?" I hissed to Rumi, who was sitting next to me with his legs sprawled out into the aisle. Total tripping hazard.

"Dunno, I wasn't paying attention." He stared down at

his phone, hidden under his desk, his fingers swiping across the screen. "Fucking sus," he muttered.

"Thanks for nothing." Adjusting my black-framed glasses on my nose, I turned to the girl on the other side of me to ask her the same question.

Yeah, glasses. Lena had been right. I only needed them for reading, but already my headaches had disappeared.

"We need to read chapter twelve and pick an essay topic from the list he posted on the student portal," the girl told me, twisting the ends of her long golden hair around her finger and staring at me from beneath her lashes. "If you're looking for a study partner, I'm available."

Before Lena, I would have been all over that. This girl was pretty, interested, and available.

"Thanks for the offer, but I'm good," I told her.

I didn't want anyone else anymore.

Just Lena.

Fuck it. I was done with playing around. Why were we wasting time when we both wanted this? Wanted to be together? Lena Drummond was mine, and it was time she knew it.

Although we'd texted each other on and off through the week and discussed Martin Smith, I didn't get a chance to see Lena in person again until Sunday. We needed to have a proper conversation about us, and it wasn't something I wanted to do over the phone.

Sunday was pouring with rain, but Cassius was in a great mood. Good thing, since it was his surprise Sunday lunch, and I was the one who was supposed to be getting him to his parents' house. We were still over two weeks away from his birthday, but last year his celebrations had stretched out over a week, so I guessed his parents were getting in there early.

As the car rumbled along the quiet streets, I glanced over at Cass before flicking my eyes back to the road. I wanted to make Lena mine, but first, I had to give him a heads-up.

"I'm gonna ask Lena to be my girlfriend. Properly. If you don't have any objections." It was easier to tell him while I was driving, and my eyes were focused on the road.

"Didn't see that coming."

My brief glance at him was enough to catch his eye roll. He fell silent after that, so I gave him time to process my statement.

Eventually, he spoke again as we were nearing our destination. "I'll say what I said before. Don't hurt her."

"I won't. And this doesn't change shit, okay? You're still my best mate, and me and Lena both have our own lives. I'm not gonna drop you."

"Okay. Good. No objections, then." There was definite relief in his voice. We pulled into the garage at his parents' house, and he grinned as I parked next to Lena's car, his mind already focused elsewhere. "Time for my surprise."

"You already knew?"

"Yep."

I shook my head, laughing. "Pretend to be surprised."

"I've been practising my shocked face in the mirror."

"Of course you have."

As I'd been instructed, I sent a text to Cassius' mum to let her know we were here. When we entered the huge dining room, Cassius immediately gasped, exaggeratedly throwing his hands to his mouth. Grinning, I looked around the room as the guests all cheered and applauded. The

Drummonds had gone all out for this "small gathering." The space was packed.

The Drummonds' dining room was pretty epic. High ceilings, smooth white marble floors, and a wall of windows along one side, showcasing the ocean view. An extendable dining table seated up to twenty people at its full length, although it looked like we weren't going to be seated at it today. The entire length was filled with food and drinks. Knowing Estella Drummond, everything would be miniature versions of normal food. And plenty of champagne, too.

"What's Jessa doing here?" I murmured to Winter when she bounded over and threw her arms around me.

"That was either Lena or her mum's idea—I can't remember. She's been having a bit of a hard time lately, I think. Did you know that Portia basically ghosted her? Fucking bitch," she muttered.

"Are you okay with her being here?" Drawing back, I stared at her, holding her lightly around the waist.

"Yeah. I'm over it. If Cade can be around James, I can be around her."

"He can barely be around James without wanting to kill him," I reminded her.

A grin tugged at her lips. "I know. It's kind of funny."

"I think James is growing on him."

"I'm not sure about that, but we can live in hope." Her voice lowered. "Anyway, enough about that. How are things going with you and Lena?"

"Ask me again tomorrow, and hopefully I'll be able to give you a different answer from the one I'd give you right now."

"Say no more." She nodded. "Good luck."

"Have you seen her?"

"She's somewhere...there." I followed the direction of her finger and saw her talking to a tall, brown-haired guy, who had his arm around the waist of a pretty woman with waist-length wavy blonde hair.

"I'm going over." Releasing Winter, I placed a kiss on her cheek, then started in the direction of Lena.

"Weston!" My progress was halted by Kinslee, clasping a glass of champagne in one hand. She threaded the other around my waist. "Hi."

Glancing over Kinslee's shoulder, I noticed Lena watching us. Her eyes darkened, narrowing as she focused on Kinslee's grip around my waist.

"Good to see you, Kins. I'll catch up with you later, yeah?" Disentangling myself from her, I closed the rest of the distance between me and Lena, watching the guarded jealousy in her eyes morph to heat as she drank me in.

There's my girl.

Reaching her, I pulled her into me with one hand, dropping a kiss on her head, and grinning at her startled intake of breath.

"Are you gonna introduce us, baby?"

My grin grew bigger as her eyes widened at my use of the word "baby," her mouth opening and closing a few times before she visibly gathered herself. "Um, yeah. This is Marcus, my cousin, and his girlfriend, Ashley. Guys, this is Weston. My...he..."

"Her boyfriend," I finished, shaking Marcus' hand before pressing a kiss to the back of Ashley's.

"My boyfriend..." Her voice came out scratchy, and she stared at me with huge eyes, unsure.

"Yep."

"We'll be back." Ducking out from under my arm, she grabbed my hand and dragged me towards the dining room exit. I let her tug me along, amused by her reaction. Everything about this girl entertained me.

Once we were out of sight of the party, in the quiet hallway, she jumped on me.

Her lips were on mine, and I opened for her as we devoured each other's mouths with hot, hungry kisses, like we'd never stop, never get enough. Her legs wrapped around my waist, and I pushed her back against the wall for extra support as she ground her body against me.

A pained hiss escaped her, and I tore my mouth away, breathing heavily. "What's wrong?"

"Nothing. Handle. Hurt my back."

Fuck. I thought I'd been pressing her against a wall, but it had been a door. I placed her down, spinning her to see the red mark on her bare back. It was faint, but I didn't like the thought of her hurting. Dropping into a crouch, I kissed it, and she sighed.

"This dress doesn't do much for back protection, does it?" I pressed another kiss to her bare skin, sliding my hands up her thighs. She trembled under my touch, her skin pebbling as I continued to kiss her while I stroked my hands higher. "But it's sexy as fuck on you." It wasn't something Lena would usually wear—silky, backless, and hitting her mid-thigh. Black, though, of course.

"I wore it for you," she said in a breathy voice. "Wanted you to notice me."

"Mmm, did you?" My hands moved higher, and I slid one between her legs and inside her underwear, feeling her slick and ready for me. "I notice you whatever you wear. Wear whatever you like."

She moaned as I curled a finger into her hot little pussy. I was so fucking hard now, it was almost painful.

"You know what I like best?" Removing my finger, I

248

straightened up and turned her to face me. "You with nothing on at all." I took my finger into my mouth, watching as her pupils dilated so much that the blue almost disappeared, swallowed by her lust for me, for us.

Her mouth opened, and she reached up to align her mouth with my ear, her whole body trembling. "I need you. Now."

38

lena

"Fuck, yes." His hands palmed my ass, pressing me into his hardness. I could barely think. When he'd said that one word, "boyfriend," and looked at me with so much possessiveness, everything had changed. I had to have him. Never mind that we were in the middle of a party for Cassius, and his sister and best friend were sneaking out. The overriding need to make him mine, make me his, was the only thought in my mind.

I'd been too crazed to think straight, and I couldn't wait any longer to have him. Fuck the party, fuck everyone else, I needed to fuck him now or I was going to lose my mind. "Now," I panted.

A dubious expression flickered across the lust on his face. "Not here."

"Fuck," I groaned, impatience threading through my tone. "The bedroom's too far."

"Hold on to me, baby." He lifted me back into his arms and carried me down the corridor, further into the house, away from the party. He paused to lower me to the ground and press me up against the wall, his hands palming my breasts as he kissed down my neck, driving me completely insane with need. I'd never been so turned on in my life, never knew this all-consuming fire for someone, to the point where nothing else existed but him.

Him, him, *him*.

This wasn't like the other times. This was new. And I craved more of it.

When he picked me back up, I kissed every part of him I could reach, needing to taste, to touch, to melt into him. I was completely oblivious to our surroundings, so when the sound of the rain suddenly became louder and he laid me back on a soft surface, I jolted.

"This." His palms slid my dress up my thighs. He lowered his head and lightly nipped at my skin. "This was where." His tongue licked over the bite. "I first kissed you." His mouth landed on my clit, and he sucked through the thin fabric barrier, making me cry out.

Who cared that we were outside and someone could walk out and catch us? Not that it was likely in this downpour, but it was a possibility.

"West," I begged, gripping his hair and tugging. "I don't want you to tease. I want you."

He raised himself onto his elbows. "You want my cock?"

"*Yes.*"

Our eyes connected, and I let him see everything.

His pupils dilated, and he inhaled a shaky breath; then he was tugging off his shirt, throwing it off to the side, and unzipping his trousers, ridding himself of the rest of his clothes. "Look at what you do to me." He gripped his cock, running his thumb over the head.

I couldn't even formulate a reply. Kicking off my shoes, I

stood on shaking legs, my feet sinking into the cushions. Wasting no time, I pulled my dress over my head and impatiently tugged off my underwear.

"This fucking view." Weston's cock jerked in his grip as he stared up at me. Suddenly, he was pulling at my legs, tugging me back down, and then his body was on top of mine. "*Lena*."

I lost myself in him. The slide of his body against mine, his hot, bruising kisses, the touch of his hands, and then, finally, the head of his cock was against me, and he thrust inside.

I bit down on his shoulder as I cried out, the stretch and burn of him filling me sending waves of pleasure through my body. "Fuck me hard. Don't hold back."

His eyes flashed, and a savage growl tore from his throat before he moved, pounding in and out of me.

"Oh, fuck." My eyes rolled back in my head as I met him thrust for thrust. He angled his body without warning, his powerful arms pushing him further up my body, and I cried out again at the sudden friction against my clit.

"So. Fucking. Good," he panted between thrusts. "Fuck."

Somewhere in the back of my consciousness, I heard a rumble of thunder, and the rain became a deluge, ricocheting off the tiles and providing a background symphony as Weston owned me with his body.

My nails dug into his ass as our bodies slid against each other, moving higher and higher until I fell apart, clenching around his cock with a shattering climax. I was still trembling against him when he came, his eyes rolling back as he lost himself in pleasure, his cock jerking and spilling deep inside me.

"Wow," I said when I'd finally regained enough brain function to form words. "Wow."

"Fucking wow." He withdrew from me, then rolled onto his back, pulling me on top of him. His fingers stroked down over my hair and onto my back. "You all good?"

I smiled at his concern. "So good. So, so good."

"I like this benefit of having a girlfriend. Sex on tap."

"You think? I'm gonna make you work for it." I kissed him, feeling him smile against me, before I laid my head on his shoulder, allowing him to wrap his arms around me and just hold me close. After a couple of minutes, though, I raised my head. "We should probably get back to the celebrations. Once we've cleaned up."

"Yeah, we should."

I rubbed at a black mark on his cheek. "I got my makeup on you, too. Sorry."

"I got my cum on you." He smirked. "And I'm not sorry about that."

"Of course you're not." I rolled my eyes. After kissing him one more time, just because I could, I moved off him. He crawled off the cushions, out of the sheltered area we'd been under, into the rain. Standing completely naked, he tipped his head back, a wide grin on his face. He looked so happy that my heart skipped a beat. And when he lowered his head to direct that smile at me, my breath caught in my throat.

He tilted his head back again, and then a few seconds later he swore angrily and swiped at his eye. "Fucking rain went in my eye." He pouted, and I couldn't help my laugh.

"Idiot," I teased. "Come back here under the shelter."

He shook his head, droplets flying everywhere. "Nah, I like this. It's refreshing."

"I'll take your word for it." I began the hunt for my clothes, when his low taunt reached my ears.

"Too scared to join me?"

"What's it worth?"

Raising his arms, he pointed to himself. "The chance to get up close with your boyfriend's sexy body?"

"One could never accuse you of modesty," I told him, but I abandoned my hunt for my clothes. Steeling myself against the pouring rain, I threw myself at him. His lips slid against mine as his arms came around me.

"Mmm. This is refreshing."

"I told you." He flashed me a smug smile that faded as his hand grasped the back of my neck, tilting my head while his other brushed my hair out of the way. "Tastes refreshing, too." One slow lick down my throat as he chased the raindrops.

"West." I could feel his cock thickening against me. "I want to carry this on." Ugh, why did I have to be the sensible one? This wasn't me. "We need to go inside. Think of Cass."

He jerked back from me. "Never mention him again when we're naked. Never."

"It's a deal. But we should go inside."

"I know." He placed a kiss to my forehead. "You go first, and I'll see you back in the party once we're both cleaned up."

"Okay." After one last kiss, I stepped back, out of the rain.

When I returned to the party, Weston was already there. It had taken me a while to sort my hair out, since the rain had made it all frizzy and I really didn't want to have to explain why it was in that state. It was now piled on top of my head. I had to change my dress, too, since I also didn't want to have to explain the mark on my back.

The dress had worked its magic anyway. I still couldn't quite believe that Weston had officially claimed me as his girlfriend. Happiness bubbled up inside me, leaving me with a permanent smile on my face.

I raided my mum's huge walk-in wardrobe—she had hundreds of dresses, and although she was shorter than me, I knew I'd find something suitable. So here I was, in yet another black dress, only this one covered my back and was even shorter than my original one.

Weston was standing by the windows, talking to Caiden, with a glass in hand. He beckoned me over, so I made my way to them, detouring to grab my own drink on the way. When I reached him, he threaded his fingers through mine, pulling me closer.

Caiden stared at us with raised eyebrows. "What's all this about?"

West shrugged. "What? Me holding my girlfriend's hand?"

"Girlfriend, huh?" He grinned, pleased. "My little brother got himself a girlfriend."

"Less of the little. I'm the same height as you, thanks."

Cade ruffled his hair. "Yep. But I'm still the older, responsible one."

"The boring one, you mean."

"There's nothing boring about me. Isn't that right, Snowflake?" He smirked at Winter, who had wandered over to join us. Her eyes flicked down to my hand, joined with Weston's, and she squeezed my arm lightly with a smile on her face, before turning her attention to Caiden.

"You're far from boring." She leaned in to kiss him. "Except when you watch *Top Gear*. That can get kind of boring."

He huffed. "We'll have to agree to disagree. Anyway, I'm happy for you both. How's Cass taken the news? Or haven't you told him yet?" Caiden addressed the question to me, but it was Weston who answered.

"I told him on the way over. He took it well. I think." He looked like he was about to say something else, when his phone sounded in his pocket. "That better fucking be Xenon," he muttered, his attention suddenly diverted to the issue that was still hanging over our heads: the dog fighting and Martin Smith.

I took his drink so he could check his phone, all of us falling silent as he read the message. "It's not Xenon—it's my program sending me an alert. I've got it automatically flagging up Martin Smith's data. Listen to this email."

In a low voice, he read from the screen.

"Thom. Funds transferred from AH. M."

"Fuck." Caiden scrubbed his hand over his face. "We'd better mention this to Dad."

"I agree." Weston shoved his phone back in his pocket. "If he's using Alstone Holdings, then he needs to be stopped."

The atmosphere turned heavy. We needed to get this guy.

"Can I have everyone's attention?"

We were pulled from our thoughts by the sound of my dad tapping a glass, standing in the centre of the room.

"As you all know, we're here to celebrate my son's birthday. Cassius? Where are you?"

Cassius was standing off to the side, close to the buffet table, chatting to Kinslee. At his dad's words, his head shot up, and a beaming smile crossed his face. He joined our dad in the centre of the room, and someone dimmed the lights. Although it was daytime, the sky was dark thanks to the heavy rain outside.

"On three. Let's sing Happy Birthday to Cassius!"

He counted to three, and everyone began to sing as my mum entered the room with a huge birthday cake balanced in her hands, with two candles on the top. I covered my mouth to hide my smile, because my mum had put me in charge of ordering the cake.

Cassius didn't miss a beat, blowing out the candles and grinning hugely as everyone cheered, but then his eye caught mine, and I knew that he was aware of who had chosen his cake.

I wandered over to him when everyone had gone back to mingling with each other. Weston came, too, his fingers threaded through mine, the feeling so natural it was like we'd been together for years.

"This is your doing, huh?" Cassius raised a brow, looking between me and the cake.

"Yep. Quite a good likeness, isn't it?"

Weston snorted with amusement. "It looks like...if a cartoon version of Cass was run over by Z's bike and half his face is melting off."

"Then the bakery did their job," I said in satisfaction. I'd asked them to give me a badly decorated *Nailed It!* version of my brother's likeness—and they'd done it perfectly.

"Tastes fucking amazing," Cassius told me through a mouthful of cake. "Great job, sis."

"You're welcome."

My cousin called to him, and he headed away, leaving me with Weston next to the cake. He stared down at it, still grinning, then pulled his phone from his pocket. "Let's commemorate our relationship status with a selfie of you with this cake."

39

weston

I checked my phone with a grin. The selfie I'd taken with Lena yesterday hadn't gone unnoticed. It seemed like most people were fans of me and Lena being together. In the photo I was trying (and failing) to feed her a piece of Cassius' birthday cake, and she was laughing as I took the photo, dropping bits of cake all over the floor. Now everyone knew she was mine.

We'd celebrated all night, wrapped up in each other, until I'd eventually left her bed in the early hours of the morning. She had school, and I had lectures in the morning, plus an essay that I wasn't even close to finishing.

Fuck, I wanted to wake up with her. She only had a couple of months left at school, and then we'd have the whole summer. I couldn't fucking wait. And after the summer, she'd be starting at Alstone College.

I made it through my morning lectures on autopilot, my mind turning from my girlfriend to Martin Smith. Caiden and I had arranged a meeting with our dad later in the day, and maybe we'd get lucky. Maybe.

Heading into the packed cafeteria at lunchtime, I

spotted my boys with Winter and Kinslee at our favourite table in front of the windows. After grabbing a sandwich and a bottle of water, I made my way over to them, taking the seat opposite my brother, who had Winter perched on his lap.

"Ready for later?" I spoke around a mouthful of bread, and Winter pulled a face at me.

"What is it with you and Cassius and your gross eating habits?"

I shrugged. Swallowing, I uncapped my bottle of water and took a swig, before glancing over at my brother. "Did you hear from Dad?"

"Yeah. All sorted," he assured me.

Nodding, I grinned at him. I had confidence in us, in what we'd planned to do. Now my dad was involved, it was actually a weight off my mind. Thanks to his help, we were going to be able to access information that we wouldn't have had a chance to get hold of before.

"Looking good, Z."

My gaze swung away from my brother to see Portia standing at our table, then flicked to Winter in time to see her baring her teeth. Blanking Portia, she pointedly turned away, and Cade wrapped his arms more tightly around her, kissing her neck.

Zayde, meanwhile, acted like he hadn't even heard her. She was beautiful, there was no doubt about it, but there was no love lost between them. Between her and any of us, for that matter.

Before Portia could respond, her attention went to someone behind me, and her eyes narrowed, a vindictive gleam coming into them. "You're not welcome here," she called.

The whole cafeteria seemed to fall silent, and I sat back

to watch this shitshow play out. Spinning in my chair, I took in the person she was addressing.

Her ex-best friend, Jessa, who was standing, frozen to the spot, tray in hand and her eyes wide.

"Fuck this," Winter suddenly mumbled, swinging herself off Caiden's lap and standing. Kinslee wasn't far behind her. I watched, open-mouthed as she stormed up to Portia. "You're. Not. Welcome. Here." Every word was punctuated by a jab into Portia's chest, and I would've laughed if I hadn't known how overdue this was.

"Get the fuck out of here." Kinslee came to stand next to Winter, her arms crossed across her chest.

Portia stared between them, blinking like she couldn't quite believe what was happening, before she decided to cut her losses and turned on her heel, making a point of sauntering out, flicking her red hair and swaying her hips.

Winter threw herself back into Cade's lap, inhaling a shaky breath. "I can't believe that just happened."

He grinned, placing a kiss on top of her head. "I fucking love you, Snowflake."

"Where did Jessa go?" Kinslee slid back into her own seat, reaching out for her bottle of Sprite and taking a sip.

"Dunno, but I wonder what happened between them. I heard my mum saying that the De Witts had fallen out with the Thompsons, so it might've been something to do with their parents," Cassius said.

"Probably pissed off that Lars De Witt went into business with Alstone Holdings." Cade shrugged. "Whatever, I don't wanna talk about Portia anymore."

"Me neither. I need to finish up my essay before we meet Dad. Meet you out the front?" Standing, I swung my bag onto my shoulder.

"See ya later."

Two hours later, my essay was done and submitted via the student portal, and I was ready to go. As I left Alstone College to meet up with Caiden, my phone rang, Lena's name flashing up on the screen.

"Hi." I heard the smile in her voice. "I just thought I'd wish you luck."

"Thanks. I'm hoping we don't need it, but I'll keep you updated." Sliding behind the wheel of my car, I checked my rear-view mirror before starting up the engine. "Come over later?"

Her voice went all soft. "Yeah."

"Good. Talk to you later." We said goodbye, and then I turned my car in the direction of my dad's office.

This time, security was expecting us, and after being issued with passes, we were ushered straight up to the floor my dad's office was on. His secretary greeted us—neither Caiden nor I ever learned their name, because they didn't always last long, but we both gave her a polite hello before entering his office.

When we entered, he was placing his desk phone back down, a look of despair on his face. "Your cousin." He sighed.

"I'm assuming you mean Roman. What's he done now?" Caiden threw himself into a chair, looking amused. Our younger cousin, Roman Cavendish, had a bit of a reputation. He attended Hatherley Hall, an exclusive boarding school up in the Cotswolds, while my aunt and uncle worked overseas.

"You don't want to know." My dad groaned, rubbing his brow. "Something to do with arson, from what I can gather. Why my sister insists on involving me, I don't know. I suppose I shall have to call the school board, yet again."

"Good luck with that." Caiden laughed, conveniently forgetting that he used to give my dad just as much grief when he attended Alstone High.

"We have approximately six minutes." My dad steered the conversation away from the touchy subject of my cousin and on to the reason for Caiden's and my presence. "I've called Martin in for an appraisal. If I'd called it a meeting, we would have run the risk of him bringing his laptop. You should have around thirty minutes to get the data, if all goes to plan."

"Never expect a plan to go as planned," Caiden cut in. "We'll be as quick as we can."

With Martin Smith occupied, we headed down the corridor to his office. We had to take care not to be seen, but thankfully this corridor only housed a small number of executive offices. We were lucky that Martin Smith didn't have his own secretary—not in here, at least. He shared his with two other members of staff, and their secretary's desk was out in the main room where a number of the lower-level employees worked.

The door was locked, but we had the pin code thanks to my dad, so that was soon taken care of. Inside, my eyes swept the sparsely furnished room, zeroing in on the sleek laptop that rested on his desk.

As we'd agreed earlier, Caiden kept watch while I got to work.

The laptop was locked, but I'd brought the solution with me. A small USB key that slotted into one of the ports on the side, it would bypass the security and, if all went well, copy the details of his hard drive across to the key. I'd written the program myself and tested it, so I was crossing my fingers that all would go well. I'd expected the laptop to have additional layers of security if it had sensitive information, so I just had to hope I'd done enough to get it to work.

I fitted it into the port and hoped for the best.

Thank fuck this wasn't like one of those movies, where a random alarm would start blaring and a big message would appear on the screen saying ACCESS DENIED. Just the opposite—the computer unlocked straight away, and the program got to work.

1 hour 23 seconds remaining...

What the fuck? I let out a groan.

"What's wrong?" Caiden hissed.

"It's saying—"

15 minutes 45 seconds remaining...

"Never mind, it just thought it would scare the fuck out of me for a second."

Caiden blinked, shrugging, then returned his attention to the doorway.

After the longest fifteen minutes of my life, the program had completed its task, and I quickly removed the USB key and pocketed it. Careful not to touch the laptop keys with my fingers, I used the sleeve of my hoodie to lock the screen again.

"Do you think we have time to search his desk?" I wondered.

"No. Dad's done that already. I'm sure he said that was one of the first things he did. Let's get out of here." Caiden motioned me towards the door, so I straightened up, and with one final glance around the room to make sure every-thing was in place, I joined him back in the hallway, locking the door behind us.

There were security cameras, but I'd already taken care of those remotely. Not that I expected Martin Smith to be browsing random footage from the middle of a Monday afternoon, but you could never be too careful.

Mission accomplished, we got out of there.

40

lena

Thursday evening, and it appeared that West had been lucky and been able to get away with copying the data undetected. Martin Smith's laptop had thrown up some interesting information. So far, nothing incriminating, yet. But what we *had* found was a series of deleted messages and recovered internet browser history that had given us enough clues that I was certain we could figure out the missing puzzle pieces.

While Weston took care of getting into import and export records, my trail of breadcrumbs led me deep into the dark web to a social network buried under other layers, undetectable but disguised in plain sight. In short, you wouldn't be able to find it unless you knew what you were looking for, but once you knew it was there, it was kind of obvious.

I'd taken care to use every shielding technique I knew, tracking and backtracking, constantly erasing my digital footprint. When I hit the network I was looking for, I registered using fake details (I highly doubted there were many people using their real details), and I was in.

Imagine a Facebook on steroids, with zero censors, and this was pretty much it. I followed the trail to a group, simply called Dogfighting UK, and clicked to join, and then I was in.

Fucking jackpot of all jackpots. I'd hit the mother lode. Scrolling through the group, I saw there were countless photos, videos, stats about different dogs, dates and details of events that were taking place, and discussions on breeders, transports...in short, a whole lot of incriminating evidence.

I didn't even want to take screenshots, in case I was somehow detected, so instead, I documented the evidence through use of my phone camera and notes, concentrating on anything I could find relating to the more local fights. The group was fairly large, but that was to be expected from a national group. Only a small number actually seemed to be southern England–based, but I took down the few details that I could find.

Before I signed out, I found a post that seemed to be a noticeboard, and I saw that someone who went by Thom had arranged to purchase three pit bull terriers from a guy based in Romania. I noted down the date, which matched with the message we'd found on Martin's phone, weeks earlier, and got out of there.

This was what we needed to intercept. Intercepting a fight itself was too risky, with the number of spectators and people involved. But if we could intercept the actual transaction of dogs, especially if they were pit bulls, a banned breed in the UK, then we might be able to stop them.

As I sat and went back through the information I'd found in the group, I pulled up the transcripts of the conversations from Martin Smith's hacked phone. It was easier to read through a transcript and look for connections, rather than replaying the voice recordings over and over again. What I couldn't work out, though, was why this Thom guy was involved, and what, if any, his connection to Martin Smith actually was. There didn't seem to be any communication between them. The only communication I'd been able to track with any regularity was that between Martin Smith and Jaroslaw Milosz, in relation to money. It all seemed to be cash, so there was no paper trail to be found.

There had to be something we were missing, and I hoped that West would be able to find it with the rest of the hacked data from Martin Smith's laptop.

As if he knew I'd been thinking of him, my phone buzzed with a message.

West: Any breakthroughs?

I sent him a message to say I'd forward him the information I had and then continued going back over the transcripts. What were we missing?

I'd sorted the conversations into personal, work-related, and potential links to the dog fighting or the money disappearance. His personal calls were almost non-existent, unsurprisingly, since outside of work and the dog fighting, he seemed to keep to himself.

That all changed about an hour later.

Finally, I had the breakthrough I'd been hoping for.

Only, it wasn't what I'd expected.

I replayed the call to Martin Smith's phone again as I shot out of the garage, aiming for Weston's house.

"Sweetheart? I told you not to call me on this number. No one can know about us." He sounded annoyed.

"Except for emergencies, you said." The voice at the other end was soft and female. "I couldn't get hold of you."

"That's because I turned my phone off. I was in a meeting, for goodness' sake!"

Oh, he was definitely getting angry.

"Marty, please."

Marty? I snorted.

"What is it?" Now he sounded resigned.

"Jaroslaw's in trouble."

He hissed. "Are you alone? I don't want anyone overhearing you."

Her tone took on a haughty note. "Marty, I'm not stupid. Of course I'm alone."

"Wait a moment." There was the sound of shuffling and a door closing before he came back on the line again. "Alright. Continue."

"Jaroslaw was almost caught by border control. He thinks they're onto him, and worse, that they got his plates. He switched vehicles, and he's laying low for the night in case there's anyone on his tail, but he wants to get rid of the cargo as a matter of urgency."

"This is not good," Martin muttered. "I have buyers lined up. We have three champions coming over on that shipment."

"I know. We need to reschedule the trade for tomorrow."

There was silence for a moment. "That shouldn't be an issue. It's only a day sooner than planned. We'll have to discount the buyers for the inconvenience, of course, but it's a small price to pay."

"I agree." Her voice lowered. "Would you prefer to

discuss this in person? My parents are out, and I have this whole big house all to myself."

A groan escaped him, making me shudder with revulsion. Gross. "Give me an hour, sweetheart."

The call ended abruptly then. There was something familiar about the female voice, something I couldn't quite place. I pulled over the side of the road when a thought hit me. Maybe James would recognise it. He'd investigated the dog fighting with me in the past, after all.

He didn't answer his phone, so I used my phone software to record the first part of the message and forwarded it to him, asking if he recognised the voice. That done, I switched my engine back on to continue to Weston's house.

At the next set of traffic lights, I checked my phone while I was waiting for them to turn green. There was a text from James with one word.

Everything suddenly became clear to me.

Thom wasn't a man.

She was a woman.

And I knew where she lived.

The lights had long turned green by the time I'd programmed the address into my satnav. I knew that everyone called me reckless and impulsive, but there was no way I was passing up this chance to catch her with Martin Smith. I wasn't planning to do anything, anyway. Just to get visual confirmation of them together, before I headed over to Weston's house. I had a feeling that this was the kind of thing everyone would need visual proof of. I could hardly wrap my head around it as it was.

Stashing my car next to the gated entrance to a field and

hoping no one would see it, I slipped through the shadows until I reached the large Georgian manor house. It was similar to the one Arlo Cavendish lived in, although on a smaller scale. Less security, too, from what I could see in my brief scan of the area.

All I needed was to get a photo, and then I could leave.

The property was bordered by a stone wall that was low enough to scale. Just. Sneaking through the field that was situated to the left, I took a running jump, my fingers closing over the top of the wall.

Okay, it was higher than I thought. My fingers scrabbled for purchase, and I felt myself slipping. Using all my strength, I managed to pull myself to the top, collapsing against the rough stone with my legs either side of the wall.

Once I had my breath back, I looked over at the house. No sign of movement. She'd said she was alone, so I took her at her word. Sprinting across the manicured lawn, I found myself a hiding place in the shadows and settled back to wait.

While I was waiting, I sent Weston a text.

Me: I'll be a bit late. Had to make an unscheduled stop
West: What? Where? You'd better not be doing anything dangerous
Me: It's not. Promise. Guess where I am?
West: Knowing you? Somewhere shady
Me: I'm insulted
West: No you're not

Laughing to myself, I forwarded him the recording of the phone call to Martin Smith, then sent another text.

Me: Listen to the recording I sent you and see if you can work it out
West: Now isn't the time to play games
Me: Listen to it

His reply came through a few minutes later.

West: A woman? How did we miss this?
Me: Do you know who she is?
West: No

A set of headlights swung into the driveway, and I crouched lower, shielding my phone screen. Before I turned my screen off and my camera on, I sent one last message.

Me: Play it to the others. Bet they can work it out

The car came to a stop, and the front door opened. The woman stood there to greet Martin, her red hair bathed in the warm light that spilled out from inside the house, turning it a burnished gold.

I angled my camera towards Martin, watching as he exited the car. His severe features softened as he looked at her standing there waiting for him.

"Marty," she said, her lips curving into a smile.

He closed the distance between them, pulling her into his arms. Their lips met.

When they drew apart, he looked down at her, grasping her chin in his hand.

One word left his lips.

"Portia."

41

weston

There was deathly silence in the lounge when I finished playing the recording. Caiden and Zayde exchanged disbelieving glances, and Cassius frowned, rubbing his brow like he couldn't believe what was happening.

"Play it again?" Winter said at last, her tone hesitant.

When it had finished playing for the second time, Cade finally spoke up. "That sounds like Portia. A whole fucking lot."

"It can't be, can it? She's like, nineteen. And Martin Smith is, what? In his fifties?" Winter glanced up at Caiden for confirmation, and he nodded, pulling a face.

"If it is her, I see why they wanted to keep it quiet."

Winter stood, pacing up and down, deep in thought. "Why haven't there been any signs? There must be some-thing we missed. Can we play that video Lena took at the party again? You know, the one where she recorded the room of people watching the dog fight."

"Yeah. I'll get my laptop." When I returned to the

lounge, I connected my laptop to the TV and played back the video frame by frame, scouring it to see if there was anything we'd missed.

"There." Winter suddenly pointed at the screen. "Could that be her?"

Sliding my glasses on, I zoomed in on the still of the video. "It's possible. Hard to tell, really." The image showed Martin Smith, staring over at Christine. Over to the right of the screen, past Christine, was what looked like the back of a head with red hair, partially obscured by a balding man. "If it is her, Martin could be looking at her, not at Christine. I don't think we can say for definite, though."

"There goes that plan, then." Winter heaved a sigh. "But if this is her, she's going to be there tomorrow. Wherever 'there' is."

"We know where it is." I remembered the info Lena had forwarded me from the dark web group. "Now we know that Martin, Portia, and Jaroslaw Milosz are all going to be there. They're the three major players, right?"

"Yeah, that's right. They mentioned the buyers, too, so we need to be careful. We don't know who these people are."

"Thom!" Cassius suddenly shouted, making everyone turn to him. "Thom... Thompson. Portia Thompson."

"Yeah, we got that, mate," Cade told him.

"Well—"

Lena came strolling in, stopping whatever Cassius was going to say. Probably for the best. Her eyes arrowed straight to mine, and her lips curved into a smile. My stomach flipped. I was so gone for this girl. *Come here*, I mouthed.

She came to me straight away, dropping down into my

lap and turning her head to speak into my ear. "You look so fucking sexy in those glasses. Just thought you should know."

"Yeah?" I kissed the side of her face, sliding my hand up her leg.

"Please. Stop."

We broke apart at Cassius' plea. I threw him an apologetic look, and he rolled his eyes in return.

"Okay. I have this." Lena was all business again, sitting up straight and tapping at her phone. "West? Just added a video to the server."

When I hit Play and it came up on the TV screen, I leaned forwards, not quite able to believe what I was seeing. I knew that Portia was involved based on what we'd just been discussing, but it was one thing knowing it and another actually believing it. Couldn't ignore the video evidence, though.

"So. Tomorrow," I began.

"Tomorrow," Lena echoed.

According to the intel we had, the exchange was set for 10:00 p.m. that night. We hadn't had any other information that would tell us otherwise, so we had to hope for the best. Cade and I had agreed not to get our dad involved in this, but we'd update him afterwards, as long as everything went to plan.

We were going in with caution. We needed video and photographic evidence, and to catch the actual exchange taking place. Proper shit that could be documented, so there was no question about who was involved.

"Remember. No confrontations. This is just about getting the evidence," I reminded everyone, catching my brother's eye as we crowded into Cassius' SUV to drive to the exchange point. Cade was sitting back and letting me take the lead on this, which honestly fucking shocked me. He gave me a reassuring nod, settling back in his seat and tugging Winter against him.

We were arriving an hour earlier than the arranged meeting time so we could scope out the place and find the best vantage points. Thanks to Google, we had an idea of the general layout, although we couldn't be sure of anything until we were actually there. I was bringing my drone—it would give us instant, up-to-date coverage which would help us with the layout and also provide additional video footage from above.

Yet another industrial area. This one was a lot more run-down than the others, and there didn't appear to be any security to speak of. No cameras, no security. Probably why they'd chosen the place. After driving around in circles for a while, Cassius pulled over next to a small, dilapidated warehouse with half a roof. All the windows had been smashed, and the walls were plastered with graffiti. After grabbing a pair of bolt cutters from the boot, he snapped the heavy-duty chain and padlock across the doors, then shoved them open, his muscles straining with the effort. The doors scraped along the ground but eventually slid open.

"Lucky I brought the bolt cutters," he commented when he hopped back in the car, looking far too pleased with himself. He drove inside, bumping over the bits of junk that littered the floor. The space was mostly empty other than the litter, except for a pile of wooden pallets stacked in one corner.

Once we were out of the car and had all our equipment in hand, we filed out of the warehouse, and Cassius closed the doors, looping the chain around them so they looked as if they were still locked.

"That'll have to do. Nowhere else to hide the car unless we want to park miles away." He took one last glance at the doors, his mouth twisting, clearly unhappy about leaving his SUV behind.

"Hey, mate. It'll be okay." Stepping up to him, I clapped my hand on his shoulder.

"Yeah. Hope so." He gave me a small smile. "Thanks."

"Come on. Let's do this."

We headed to the open area that the trade was supposedly taking place. The info had mentioned "warehouse 4" which was easy to spot, a large black painted 4 above the doors. Stopping a safe distance away, behind a stack of rusting metal crates, I launched my drone into the air, holding the controls, complete with a small viewing screen, in front of me.

My eyes were drawn to movement in the corner of the screen, and my stomach dropped.

Fuck.

"We've got problems." My voice remained calm, though inside I was fucking panicking. Everyone crowded around me, watching as figures appeared and the warehouse doors began to open.

"Everyone into position, now. We'll have to do what we can. Get as much footage as you can, but don't let yourself get fucking caught," Caiden hissed, taking over while I concentrated on directing the drone over the area, looking out for anything we might have missed.

I remained where I was, holding the drone steady, and everyone else spread out, keeping to the cover of the crates and buildings around the immediate area. We were just filming, gathering evidence, so the risk should be minimal.

Not that we could rely on anything. We'd learned that the hard way when everything had happened with Christine.

Winter stayed close, balancing her phone on the crates and setting it to film through a gap, angled at the warehouse doors. She kept up a commentary for me in a low voice, while I circled the drone higher, bringing it over the warehouse roof. I had to switch to night vision here, although it wasn't fully dark yet. When I lowered the drone to the jagged hole in the roof, it didn't pick anything up thanks to the dim interior.

"Martin and Portia have turned up together." A completely inappropriate laugh burst from her before she clamped her hand over her mouth. "Sorry. I just thought of her calling him Marty, and it made me laugh. I don't know why."

I flashed her a quick grin, before returning my attention to the screen. "What else? Looks like the lorry is inside the warehouse."

"They're going into the warehouse." She huffed. "I can't see anything else now."

I took the drone as low as I dared, almost scraping it along the roof of the lorry that took up all the fucking space inside. "We need to get closer. I can't see anything."

"Let's go. Where are the others?"

Carefully navigating the drone back out through the warehouse roof, I scanned the area. "There." I angled my head at the screen. Caiden, Zayde, and Cassius were circling the area, gradually getting closer and closer to the warehouse, their aim clear.

"Where's Lena?"

We both spoke at the same time.

Dread rose in me so fast that I couldn't catch a breath.

My whole world stopped when I heard the scream.

42

lena

I'd slipped inside the warehouse as soon as Caiden had given the order to get into position. This was where we needed to be, and I knew the others would be right behind me.

Only, they weren't right behind me. Seemed like they'd decided to err on the side of caution, scouting the outside area before getting to where the action was. Fuck that. We were wasting time.

Keeping low, I hugged the walls. It wasn't a huge warehouse, and the lorry inside took up most of the available space. Crouched in the corner, I began filming, watching as Jaroslaw Milosz exited the cab and came around to the back. It appeared that he was alone for now.

Unlocking the back doors of the lorry, he lowered a ramp, then lit up a cigarette, leaving it dangling from his mouth as he clipped the doors into place so they remained open. Whines, growls, and barks reached my ears, and I zoomed in with the camera, debating whether to get closer.

My mind was made up when Jaroslaw stepped back down the ramp and headed outside. This was my chance.

No one else was here inside the warehouse with me. Darting forwards, I raced up the ramp and into the black interior of the lorry.

I'd come prepared with a head torch so I could keep my hands free. If only I could've used a headcam—but it wasn't worth the risk if I was caught. My phone was uploading the video to my secure server as I filmed, immediately deleting it from the phone itself. It would do that as long as my phone signal remained. There was no way I was planning on being caught, but *if* I was, I could plead innocence, and no one would be able to pin any evidence on me.

Precautions. Just as Promethium had drummed into me.

Switching on the torch, I took a moment to get my bearings, then angled my head around so the light shone into the corners. The part of the lorry I was in was stacked with boxes, so I moved deeper inside, following the noises of animals in distress.

There.

A pair of eyes stared out of the bars of a large dog carrier. I watched as the dog lunged for the bars, snapping and snarling. There was already a large smear of blood on the outside of the carrier, and I steeled myself against the sight. I knew I normally came across as confident and able to handle shit, but I'd never lose the sick feeling that bubbled up inside me every time I saw an animal suffering.

I filmed as much as I could, taking care to show the signs of distress, and the chalk markings that denoted which dogs were which—names followed by codes: Gr Ch, Ch, and so on, which showed how valuable they were based on the number of fights they'd won. Then there were the cages with the dogs that had already seemed to give up hope—those destined for the death matches. None of those would survive for long.

Once I'd got all the footage I needed, I slowly made my way back to the exit of the lorry, pausing at the top of the ramp when voices reached my ears. Quickly, I flattened myself against the side, keeping back and waiting to see what would happen.

"Do you have the money?" That was Jaroslaw speaking.

Portia was the one to answer, her voice all faux sweet. I nearly gagged. "Of course."

Inching forwards, I was able to see her placing her hand on his arm, while Martin kept his arm clenched around her waist. "We are discounting the buyers for the inconvenience. This is your mistake, so we will deduct 20 percent from your payment."

"No!" His rebuttal was swift and sharp.

"I'm afraid so," Martin chipped in, with the poorest attempt at a regretful expression I'd ever seen.

Jaroslaw stepped forwards, bristling, and I leaned further out from the side of the lorry so I could get a better view.

At the same time, Portia raised her head and her eyes met mine.

Horror filled her gaze.

And then she *screamed*.

43

weston

The scream reverberated around the area, making everyone freeze. Then there was a loud, masculine shout, and I was gone. Thrusting the drone controls at Winter, I scaled the crates, jumping off the other side and landing heavily on the cracked concrete. I made a run for the warehouse, uncaring about the need to be cautious. The *only* thing that mattered was getting to Lena.

From behind me I heard a shout, but I paid it no attention, running headlong straight into the warehouse. My eyes took everything in an instant—a screaming Portia pointing a finger up the ramp, Jaroslaw Milosz leaping inside, and Martin Smith being completely fucking useless and just standing there, opening and closing his mouth like a fish.

I had no plan, no weapon. All I knew, based on the information my brain had processed as I entered the warehouse, was that Lena was inside that lorry.

My feet pounded up the ramp, and I leapt inside.

"Lena?"

"Stay there." Her voice seemed to echo around us. She

fell silent, and I listened. The dogs were getting louder, frenzied, and it was impossible to hear anything else. Then, she was there, next to me, Jaroslaw hot on her heels. "Go!" she shouted, taking a running jump off the ramp and dropping into a forward roll.

So fucking hot.

Then Jaroslaw was on me, and he took me down with him. We rolled down the ramp, grappling with each other. Yeah, I could fight, but it wasn't like I was a trained ninja or anything.

What I did know was how to fight dirty. Bringing my head back, I slammed it into his nose as hard as I could. There was a loud crunch, and blood began pouring from his nose. He screamed, a combination of pain and rage, and twisted us both, knocking us off the side of the ramp. My shoulder slammed into the sharp metal edge, and the sudden pain made me lose focus. I landed on my back with a jarring impact, my head smacking into the floor.

Dazed, I watched as a savage Lena came up behind Jaroslaw, swinging a thick, heavy chain in her hands. She launched herself onto his back, wrapping the chain around his throat and yanking, hard. A gagging sound came from his throat as blood continued to spurt from his nose, and as she kept up the pressure, his struggles slowed until he fell limp, still breathing but unconscious.

"West!" Lena was suddenly in front of me, cradling my face in her hands. "Are you okay?"

'Y-yeah," I croaked out. "Are you?" I reached up to touch the side of her face, to reassure myself she was still here with me.

She smiled, a smile of relief, tears gathering in her eyes. "I'm okay."

I struggled into a sitting position, ignoring my pounding head and throbbing arm. "Come here."

She crawled into my lap, her body shaking, and I held her tightly. Right then, I knew *exactly* how much she meant to me.

"It's probably the wrong time to tell you this." I buried my face in her shoulder. "But I want you to know that I love you."

"What?" Drawing back from me, she stared at me, her eyes wide. "Say that again? Because I think I misheard you."

"I said..." Stroking my thumb down her cheek, I met her gaze. "I said that I love you."

"You do?" Her voice was unsure, yet so full of hope that it made me smile.

"Yes I fucking do. It's okay if—"

She shut me up with a finger to my lips, a smile breaking out over her face. "Oh, Weston. Don't you know? I've loved you since I was eight years old. It just took you a while to catch up with me."

———

While we'd been busy with Jaroslaw Milosz, the others had not only managed to incapacitate Martin Smith and Portia, but a tearful Portia was busy confessing everything to anyone and everyone who'd listen, clearly afraid of the threat of arrest. The buyers never showed, most likely scared well away by the police presence, thanks to Winter's call to my dad. He in turn had called in one of his detective friends, who was liaising with the RSPCA to take care of the dogs, while the police dealt with Martin and Portia.

When my dad had shown up, he had a look of resignation in his eyes as he saw me seated on an upturned crate, covered in Jaroslaw Milosz's blood while Lena tended to the cut on my arm courtesy of the first aid kit that had been stashed in Cassius' SUV. He came and sat on the crate next to me, waiting until Lena had finished cleaning my wound.

"It's just a scrape," she told me, pressing a kiss to my shoulder. Her eyes went from me to my dad, and she nodded. "I'm just gonna check on my brother."

"Thanks. For, y'know." I squeezed her hand, then lifted it to my lips. She smiled, then disappeared, leaving me with my dad.

"You can say it." I waited, fully prepared for him to come down hard on me.

"I'm proud of you, Weston." He squeezed my uninjured shoulder. "So proud of you. Don't you forget it." Then he stood, leaving me gaping at him.

Before he left, he looked down at me, a small smile tugging at the corners of his lips. "Bring Lena over for dinner next week." It wasn't a question.

"Uh. Yeah. I will. Thanks, Dad."

With one last parting smile, he went off to talk with his detective friend.

One by one, the others drifted over, once the detective had spoken to each of us. First Winter, then Zayde and Caiden, then Cassius, and finally, my girlfriend. We'd agreed to turn over the evidence we had—while they couldn't use the illegal evidence in court, our footage from both tonight and the dog fight we'd attended before would be enough to build up a strong case.

Lena tugged me to my feet, wrapping her arms around my waist.

"Let's go home," I said.

Together, the six of us headed into the night.

EPILOGUE 1

weston

ONE WEEK LATER

"Ha. Look at this." Curled up in an armchair in the lounge in my house, Lena shifted in my lap, angling her phone so I could see the screen. There was a message from James Granville.

> **James:** I'm glad it's over. Let's agree to never get dragged into anything like this again

"I hate to say it, but I agree with him." I dropped a kiss on my girlfriend's head. "I'd like to just enjoy being with you for a while. Without all the other shit. No more fighting or chasing down shady guys. Just you and me."

She laughed. "A quiet life is overrated."

"Yeah. You're probably right." Stroking my fingers down her arm, I smiled as she settled back against me. "Promethium will probably have something else for us to do soon enough, anyway."

"I hope so."

I laughed at the enthusiasm in her voice. "Maybe not just yet, huh?"

She twisted around to face me, suddenly serious. "Not just yet. We have our appointment to get through, and that's gonna be..." Her words trailed off.

"Yeah." We'd booked an appointment with her therapist. Two, in fact. We were seeing the therapist together, to talk in more depth about her assault and what I could do to support her, and I had my own appointment in addition to that. I hadn't had much of a chance to come to terms with the fact that my mum's death hadn't been as it seemed, and while I'd been able to push it aside with everything else that had been going on, it had kind of hit me all over again. A couple of days ago, I'd had a long talk with my dad and brother which had helped a lot, but I wanted to talk to a professional to get things straight in my head, to work through my thoughts.

"I'm gonna be here for you," I promised her, running my fingers through her silky hair. "Whatever I can do. I just want to make you happy."

"You do. People keep asking what's wrong with me, because I'm smiling all the time." She pulled a face, making me laugh.

"I fucking love you. My badass girl."

"Is this in reference to the chain again?" Humour danced in her eyes. "Look, Jaroslaw used that chain on the dogs. It was poetic justice that I used it on him."

"You're right," I agreed.

"Anyway," she continued. "You're the one who broke his nose."

"That was so fucking satisfying." I grinned. "He deserved it."

"He did." She reached up, curling her arms around the back of my neck and tugging my head down to hers. "A kiss before we have to go?"

As soon as her lips met mine, nothing else existed.

Only her.

———

Just over fifty minutes later, we were walking through the front door of my dad's house, only ten minutes late.

It wasn't my fault that my girlfriend was so addictive.

"Nice of you to join us." Caiden smirked at me over the top of his glass. My dad, seated at the head of the long dining table, shot him a warning look.

"Take a seat." He indicated the empty chairs on either side of the table. Lena slid into the seat next to Winter, and I dragged the chair out next to my brother.

"It's not like you've ever been late to anything because you've been too busy with Winter."

"Yeah, alright." He shrugged. "You might have a point."

I grinned at him, and he rolled his eyes. Watching us both from over the top of his wine glass, my dad cleared his throat pointedly, but he was unable to hide his own grin.

The staff began serving up our food. When we were all eating, my dad told us how they'd manage to trace the Alstone Holdings discrepancies after the police had raided Martin Smith's flat and recovered sensitive information, including a paper trail that led back to Alstone Holdings. We spoke about the situation for a bit, then my dad turned to me and said something I hadn't expected to hear from him.

"Our systems have always been handled by an external company, as you know. Now, nothing is set in stone, but perhaps we should consider bringing it back in-house when you graduate, Weston."

"What?" Everyone turned to stare at him, and he smiled widely, clearly loving our shock.

"It's about time Alstone Holdings had its own proper IT department. Maybe you'd be interested in something like that? Who knows, maybe you could even come up with security systems for our properties, as well as making our own system secure."

I gaped at him, unsure of what to say. Lucky for me, he continued speaking. "I know and you know that you'll be taking your place at Alstone Holdings when you graduate. But I get the feeling that you'd much rather work with computers than with business dealings. Am I correct?"

"Yes," I managed, then, "*Fuck*, yes."

"Language," he said automatically, before turning his attention to Lena. "You too. I hear that you're very handy with computers."

"I am," she stated confidently, grinning at him. "Count me in."

"We still have plenty of time to put things into place, but I want you to know that if this is something you're interested in, we'll make it happen."

"Thanks. I'd like that." A smile spread across my face, my head already filling with ideas. Suddenly, I couldn't wait to graduate.

"Proud of you, bro." Cade squeezed my shoulder.

"Cheers. Same." I leaned over and gave him a hug, which was kind of awkward because of the angle we were sitting at, and also for the fact that he clearly wasn't expecting it. After a couple of seconds, though, he hugged me back, and then Winter was joining us, then Lena and my dad, and yeah...it turned into one of those cheesy as fuck moments where everyone hugs each other and congratulations get thrown around.

Secretly, though, I loved it.

EPILOGUE 2

lena

TWO MONTHS LATER

Somehow, Portia had managed to get out of a jail sentence, thanks to her highly paid lawyer spinning a story of her being an impressionable young girl seduced by the older man. Maybe that was true, but she was still guilty of facilitating things. My opinion didn't matter, though, because she also had enough information on Martin Smith's shady dealings to have him locked away for a long time, and the courts looked very favourably on the evidence she'd provided.

On the plus side, she'd been kicked out of Alstone College, and last I'd heard, her family was selling their house and moving to the other side of the country. The evidence I'd managed to obtain from the group on the dark web had helped to convict a number of additional people, and the dog-fighting ring had been broken up. Although I knew that it still continued on elsewhere, the fact that we'd managed to eradicate it in Alstone was a huge deal. It was something I'd been working towards for so long.

It was a gorgeous summer day, and I was reclining on the uncovered part of the deck outside the back of the Four's house, basking in my bikini in the sun's rays.

My house, too, as of this morning. I'd agreed with West and my parents that I'd trial living here over the summer, and if it didn't work out for whatever reason, I'd move into university accommodation when my first semester began in September (*not* back in with my parents. As much as I loved them, I wanted to experience new things). Plus, Winter was beyond excited to have another girl living in the house.

The buzz of my phone pulled me out of my thoughts, and I unlocked the screen to find a message from my mum.

Mum: Hope moving in went ok. Come for dinner this week, I miss you! xx
Me: I've only been gone for a day
Mum: Even so. Dinner. Wednesday? Bring my favourite son-in-law too! xx
Me: MUM. STOP.
Me: I will come, as long as you promise not to call West your son-in-law
Mum: I won't say it to his face. How's that?
Me: I guess it'll have to do. See you Weds then. Love you xx
Mum: Love you too xx

Placing my phone back on the deck, I slipped off my sunglasses and laid them on top. Then, closing my eyes, I lay back again, enjoying the sun on my face.

My eyes flew open and I shrieked as cold droplets hit my bare stomach. Weston was standing over me with a huge grin on his face, brandishing a dripping ice cube.

"You're going to pay for that," I warned, bounding off the chair and attempting to wrestle the ice cube out of his grip.

"Slippery fucker!" he shouted as the ice cube fell, landing in the grass below. Before I could dive for it, he picked me up and spun me around, carrying me back into the house.

"Where are you taking me?" Locking my legs around his waist, I buried my face in his shoulder, holding him tightly.

"I told everyone that we needed to celebrate you moving in, so we have the house to ourselves."

"We're celebrating tonight, aren't we?" My stomach flipped with the sensation that I always got around my boyfriend—the heady combination of lust and something far deeper. The connection between us was so strong that I constantly wondered how I'd managed to get so lucky. How the boy I'd always loved, loved me back.

"You know what I'm referring to." I could hear the amusement in his voice, and I smiled against him.

"I know, and I'm already sure that I'll prefer these celebrations to my housewarming party later."

"I'll make sure of it," he promised, his voice going all dark and raspy as we reached our bedroom door and he kicked it open.

"West..." Drawing my head back, I took his lower lip between my teeth, watching his pupils dilate as he stared at me.

"Fuck, Lena. You're so fucking beautiful." He pressed me up against the wall, his mouth coming down on mine. I moaned into his mouth as his tongue met mine, all hot, devastating kisses.

"I'm so fucking glad you're wearing this." Dropping me on the bed, he crawled over my body, ridding me of my bikini in what felt like seconds, before tugging off his shorts to reveal his hard cock.

He scraped his teeth down my throat, dropping soft bites, kisses, and licks down my body until I was begging, aching for him. "Need you now. *Please.*"

"Yeah?" His eyes went to half-mast, as he lowered his body, dragging his hard length along my wetness. "What if I wanna make you come before I fuck you?"

"No. Need you." Wrapping my legs around him, I used a useful trick to flip us over so I was on top of him, and then I was sinking down onto his thick cock.

"Fucking love you," he rasped, his heated eyes devouring me as our hips thrust against each other. "Touch yourself."

When my hand went to my clit, he swallowed hard. "*Oh, fuck.*" His groan had me riding him harder, our bodies chasing each other higher and higher.

Then, he was flipping us back over, pounding into me, and I shattered around him, crying out his name.

"*Weston.*"

His name on my lips sent him over the edge, his cock pulsing inside me as he shuddered against my body.

I'd never get enough of him.

When I'd recovered enough to breathe again, I whispered the words that I'd never get tired of saying to him.

"I love you." Eyes closed, I lay back, sleepy and sated. I felt him carefully withdraw from me, and then his hot breath was on my skin as he lowered his head to kiss my eyelids.

"I love you, too."

My eyes fluttered back open, and I drank in the sight of him laying soft kisses all the way down my arm. Stopping at the bottom, he pressed his lips to the inside of my wrist, where Roman numerals had been inked a couple of weeks ago.

IV.

Yeah. I was one of them now.

THE END

ACKNOWLEDGMENTS

I have so many people to thank, as usual! First up, I have to thank my son for being my alpha reader for chapter one, and informing me how an eight year old kid should actually sound (he did not read any of the rest of the book). Credit goes to him for the line about Galactus, which he forced me to add!

Huge thanks to my awesome alpha and beta readers Jenny (also for coping with my many neurosis!), Megan, Sue and Ashley. This book wouldn't be what it was without you! And to my Chicago BFF/Taylor Swift superfan Claudia, you push me every day! I love you all.

A big thank you goes to Jen and Wildfire for all your hard work and support. You make this process so much easier! And I have to mention my amazing street team and ARC team, I'm so thankful for you all.

To my awesome editing and proofreading combo of Sandra, Rumi and Sid, thank you for whipping this book into shape.

And thank you as always to you for reading, and to everyone who shares, reviews, makes edits, and all the other amazing things that the readers in the book community do.

Becca xoxo

ALSO BY BECCA STEELE

LSU Series

Blindsided (M/M)

The Four Series

The Lies We Tell

The Secrets We Hide

The Havoc We Wreak

A Cavendish Christmas (free short story)*

The Fight In Us

The Bonds We Break

Alstone High Standalones

Trick Me Twice

Cross the Line (M/M)

In a Week (free short story)*

Savage Rivals (M/M)

Boneyard Kings Series (with C. Lymari)

Merciless Kings (RH)

Vicious Queen (RH)

Ruthless Kingdom (RH)

Other Standalones

Mayhem (a Four series spinoff)*

Heatwave (a summer short story)*

London Players Series

The Offer

London Suits Series

The Deal

The Truce

The Wish (a festive short story)*

Box Sets

Caiden & Winter trilogy

*all free short stories and bonus scenes are available from https:// authorbeccasteele.com

**Key - M/M = Male/Male (gay) romance

RH = Reverse Harem (one woman & 3+ men) romance

ABOUT THE AUTHOR

Becca Steele is a USA Today and Wall Street Journal bestselling romance author. She currently lives in the south of England with a whole horde of characters that reside inside her head.

When she's not writing, you can find her reading or watching Netflix, usually with a glass of wine in hand. Failing that, she'll be online hunting for memes, or wasting time making her 500th Spotify playlist.

Join Becca's Facebook reader group Becca's Book Bar, sign up to her mailing list, or find her via the following links:

facebook.com/authorbeccasteele

instagram.com/authorbeccasteele

bookbub.com/profile/becca-steele

goodreads.com/authorbeccasteele

Printed in Great Britain
by Amazon

86070676R00185